"You've just missed your friend Mavis Owen."

Alun flashed her a wary glance, but Jessica went on curtly. "She told me about the project you and she have in mind—the adventure school."

"What did she say?"

"She said you couldn't go into partnership with her while you're married to me. Did you say that?"

"Something like that." He shrugged his shoulders.

"She said I was in your way," Jessica continued. "So I told her that I'd never get in your way if organizing a school with her was what you really wanted to do, and she asked me to tell you that. I also told her that... that if you wanted a divorce, I'd be willing to give you one."

"Thank you very much," Alun drawled.

Books by Flora Kidd

HARLEQUIN PRESENTS

HARLEQUIN ROMANCE

These books may be available at your local bookseller.

Don't miss any of our special offers. Write to us at the following address for information on our newest releases.

Harlequin Reader Service
P.O. Box 52040, Phoenix, AZ 85072-2040
Canadian address: P.O. Box 2800, Postal Station A,
5170 Yonge St., Willowdale, Ont. M2N 5T5

FLORA KIDD

the open marriage

Harlequin Books

TORONTO • NEW YORK • LONDON
AMSTERDAM • PARIS • SYDNEY • HAMBURG
STOCKHOLM • ATHENS • TOKYO • MILAN

Harlequin Presents first edition January 1985
ISBN 0-373-10756-0

Original hardcover edition published in 1984
by Mills & Boon Limited

CHAPTER ONE

'So you want to know where Alun is? Why?'

The speaker was Margian Gower. A small woman with a mobile almost monkeyish face, her well-shaped head covered with silky black curls, she was sitting before a large light-edged make-up mirror in a dressing room backstage of a theatre in the West End of London and she was preparing for her role in the revival of Emlyn Williams' spine-chiller play *Night Must Fall*.

Pausing in the act of drawing in wrinkles across her brow, Margian glanced at the reflection of the woman who was standing behind her, Jessica Martin, tall and slim, dressed in green linen, her thick golden hair cut in an attractive ear-tip-length style and curving in a deep wave across her forehead.

'I want to get in touch with him,' Jessica said coolly with a slight shrug of her shoulders as if she didn't really care whether she found out where Alun, her estranged husband and Margian's younger brother, was living.

'And you've no idea where he is right now?' exclaimed Margian.

'No.'

'But surely . . .' Margian broke off, looking puzzled.

'Alun hasn't written to me or . . . or been to see

me since . . . since . . .' Jessica paused too, biting
her lower lip.

'Since you left him?' suggested Margian with a
sardonic lift of her dark eyebrows.

'I didn't leave him. He left me,' retorted Jessica,
her eyes, which were a lovely dark blue—the
colour of glistening slate—flashed a glance at
Margian's reflection. 'He slammed out of the flat
one day and went off to New York, and I don't
even know if he ever came back to this country.'

'But that must have been nearly two years ago,'
remarked Margian. Her mouth twisted wryly. 'I
gather you quarrelled with him, and he lost his
temper before he slammed out.'

'Yes. We did quarrel,' Jessica admitted reluctantly.

'I suppose you accused him of being unfaithful
to you and he took umbrage. Sounds like Alun,'
murmured Margian, leaning forward to stare in
the mirror at her face as she added more make-up.
Slowly she was changing, becoming older-looking,
her face wrinkled and pale, beginning to look like
the upper class elderly woman she was about to
portray on the stage, except for the black curls
that rioted over her head.

Alun's hair was like that too, thought Jessica,
the only resemblance he had to his sister, and there
were glints of gold and silver in the blackness. Her
fingers clenched as if in rejection of the remembered feel of his curls winding around them.

'How do you know that's what happened?' she
demanded. 'Have you seen Alun? Did he tell you?'

'Yes, I've seen him. But he didn't tell me

anything about you and him. Knowing him as I do I just guessed.' Margian gave Jessica a rather pitying glance. 'I suppose you tried to tie him down.'

'No, I didn't.' Jessica sank down on a nearby chair. 'Ours was an open marriage. We agreed before we married to give each other the freedom to come and go as we pleased. It was working . . . or at least I thought it was working quite well, until . . . until . . .' She paused again, frowning down at her hands.

'Until what?' demanded Margian, her eyes narrowing as she studied Jessica's face.

'Until someone told me that Alun was having an affair with another woman.'

'Who told you that?'

'Sally Fairbourne.'

'And you believed her?' exclaimed Margian incredulously as she lifted a white-waved wig of hair from a dummy head on the dresser before her before setting it carefully on her head to cover her curls.

'Sally and I have been friends for years, ever since we were babies, so why wouldn't I believe her?' retorted Jessica defensively. 'And she's known Alun longer than I have. It was at her parent's home that I met him, you know.'

'I know,' sighed Margian. 'So you trust her more than you trust Alun because you've known her longer than you've known him. Oh, well, I suppose that makes some sort of sense. Why do you want to see him? To suggest a divorce?'

'Maybe.' Jessica's eyes were hidden swiftly by

their thick white lids. 'Are you going to tell me where he is?'

Margian swung round in her chair until she was facing Jessica. With shrewd dark brown eyes she stared at her sister-in-law. Jessica was thinner than when she had last seen her. The English schoolgirl bloom had gone. Jessica was now a striking-looking woman of nearly twenty-five, self-assured, well-dressed, and accustomed probably to all the good things in life; the best hotels to stay in when she travelled for the furniture company she worked for; the best food, the best clothes; all the comforts of life, in fact. Margian's lips curved cynically and in the depths of her dark eyes mischief glinted briefly.

'All right, I'll tell you where Alun is,' she said. 'But if you do get in touch with him you're not to tell him I told you where he is. He's at Whitewalls—that's the house where our father lived most of his life and where he was born. The house where Alun and I lived when we were children. The house where Gowers have lived for generations, rearing sheep and writing poetry. What else could they do in wild Wales?' Margian's voice was mocking.

'Why is he living there?' exclaimed Jessica.

'Writing. A biography of our father, one of the most distinguished of Welsh poets and men of letters,' replied Margian, sadness making her eyes seem even darker. 'Did you ever meet him? Did you ever meet Huw Gower?'

'Yes, I did. I met him when he came to London to do a poetry reading for the B.B.C. Alun and I

met him off the train and took him to his hotel,'
said Jessica, remembering a tall man with wild
white hair adrift above his craggy cliff-like face.
He had looked at her with kindly dark brown eyes
and then had said something in Welsh to Alun.

'What did your father say to you at the station?'
she had asked Alun later the same evening. 'It was
about me, wasn't it?'

'He was quoting from a poem by Dafydd ap
Gwilym, a Welsh poet who lived in the Middle
Ages,' Alun had told her. They had been in bed at
the time, making love, and he had been stroking
her nightgown away from her, worshipping her
body with his hands. 'Dad said you reminded him
of some lines written by Dafydd.'

'What lines? Can you translate them for me?'
she had asked.

'I'll try,' he said, and then had continued slowly,

The gentle girl with the golden hair,
Golden is the burden that you carry on your head.
White is your body and slim,
And you shine with it. What a gift!'

'Dad was right,' Alun had continued. 'You are
gentle and your hair is golden and your body is
white and slim, shining, a gift for me.'

Resonant and lilting, Alun's voice had woven a
spell of romance about her as he had leaned over
her, dark-browed, and she had responded, as she
always had, to his lovemaking, her shy soul
flattered and warmed by what he had said about
her, her body expanding and lifting to his touch.

She became aware, with a start, of the reality of

the dressing room, the smell of greasepaint, the
heat of many light-bulbs, of Margian's wrinkled
and powdered face grinning at her.

'I'm sorry,' she muttered. 'What did you say?'

'Miles away, weren't you?' Margian mocked.
'Where, I wonder?'

'I was thinking about your father,' Jessica
replied stiffly. 'I liked him. I liked his poetry too.'

'Yet you didn't go to his funeral,' retorted
Margian.

'I . . . I didn't know he had died for a while, and
Alun and you didn't invite me to the funeral.'
Jessica was still stiff, still defensive. 'Would you
please give me the address of the house in Wales
where Alun is living?'

'It's just called Whitewalls and it's near the town
of Dolgellau.' Margian pronounced as the Welsh
do—*Dol-geth-lee*. 'I don't know the postal code.
Are you going to write to him? Or are you going
to see him?'

'Write to him, I think,' said Jessica, writing
down the name of the house and the nearest town
in a small notebook she took from her handbag. 'I
don't suppose he's on the phone, is he?'

'No phone—Dad didn't like phones. Wouldn't
have one installed—said it would be an intrusion
of his privacy to have one.' Margian frowned.
'You know, Jessica, it would be best if you went to
see Alun. You might wait for ever for a letter from
him, he's notoriously bad at answering letters. Do
you have a car?'

'Mother and I share one.'

'Well, if you do decide to go and see him your

best bet is to take M1 north and branch off that on to the M6. Go as far as Cannock and from there take a cross-country route to Telford Shrewsbury, Welshpool and Dinas Mawddwy. Dolgellau is the next town. Anyone there will tell you how to get to the house of Huw Gower. He was something of a local hero, you know, ever since he was crowned bard at the Eisteddfod in Llangollen.'

'Thank you.' Jessica stood up. 'I won't take up any more of your time because I realise it's nearly time for the curtain to go up. It was good of you to see me.'

'No, not good. We Gowers are never good, at least Alun and I have never been good,' Margian's dark eyes glinted again with mischief. 'I was curious to see you. I wanted to see if you'd changed since the last time we met. All things considered you seem to have survived being separated from Alun pretty well, which makes it hard for me to believe you were once head over heels in love with him. Infatuated with him, weren't you? So much so you followed him to London and bothered him until he gave in and married you.'

'That's not true!' Jessica flared. 'Oh, you make it sound as if . . . and if I . . .'

'Importuned him?' suggested Margian dryly. 'Well, didn't you? It certainly looked like that to those of us who were watching from the wings of the theatre, so to speak. You turned up at the place where he was living then, penniless and without anywhere to stay, and threw yourself on his mercy so that he took you in, let you live in his flat and even found you a job. And then you turned round and told your father Alun had seduced you so your father insisted Alun marry you.' Margian's voice grated with scorn.

'I didn't!' gasped Jessica, losing her cool suddenly so that she looked younger and less sophisticated, her cheeks flushed pink, her lips trembling slightly as she defended herself. 'I didn't do what you say! I didn't tell my father Alun had seduced me. Alun and I were friends . . . at least I thought he was a friend, so I went to him for help.' She stopped took a deep breath and turned towards the door. 'Oh, what's the use of trying to explain to you? You're not going to believe anything I say. You've always disliked me because . . . because your brother married me. You're jealous of me.'

'No, not jealous,' replied Margian quietly and with dignity. 'But concerned—for Alun. You see, I love him very much and I'd like him to be happy. I've always thought you were too young for him, too immature, expecting too much from him, hoping he would solve your problems for you. Admit, Jessica, that's how you've always seen him as a knight in shining armour, protecting you, rescuing you from fates worse than death . . . until you found out that he's only human after all, no better and no worse than any other man?'

'I found out that he didn't love me as I loved him,' said Jessica woodenly, staring at the door panels in front of her, not daring to face Margian again in case the other woman saw the tears that had brimmed in her eyes.

'And now you've met someone who does love you, is that it?' Margian queried jeeringly. 'Someone dependable. Someone who can keep you in the comfort to which you're accustomed. Someone more suited to be a husband than a life-loving free-spirited writer like Alun?'

'Perhaps I have,' Jessica snapped. She opened the door. 'Goodbye, Margian, and thanks again.'

She closed the door sharply behind her and stood for a moment in the dimness of the passageway, sniffing a little and wiping the tears from her cheeks. When she had recovered her composure she left the theatre by the stage door and stepped out into the sun-hazed humid air of the June evening. Immediately Chris Pollet was at her side, his hand under her elbow, to guide her down the narrow side street towards Shaftesbury Avenue.

'How did you get on?' he asked. 'Was she forthcoming?'

'Yes. She gave me Alun's address.'

'Good. So now you can write to him. Or better still get your lawyer to write to him. I thought we'd eat in Soho. Italian suit you?'

She agreed, and they turned another corner into a narrow street lined with many different restaurants. In a few minutes they were stepping into the one Chris had chosen and were being shown to a table in a booth separated from the next booth by a partition of dark wood topped by red silk curtains hung on thick brass rods. After the humid warmth outside the interior of the restaurant was cool and dim. Light came from

candles flickering in red bowls on the tables that
were covered with red and white checked cloths.

They were handed menus and the waiter
departed to fetch the white wine Chris had ordered
for them to drink. Jessica stared down at the menu
but made no sense of it. The words were blurred.
She was thinking what a coincidence it was that
Chris had chosen this particular restaurant, where
she had so often come with Alun when they had
lived together. She laid the menu down and looked
across at Chris. A big fair man, he was brisk and
forceful, with a bulldoggish sort of face. He
assumed he knew what she wanted. He assumed
she would marry him if she could get a divorce
from Alun. It was his idea that she should get in
touch with Alun, write to him or get a lawyer to
write to him. He assumed too much, she thought.

'I don't have a lawyer,' she said flatly.

He looked up and across at her. His pale grey
eyes reflected the flame of the candle.

'I'm sure the company's lawyer can give you the
name of a good divorce lawyer,' he retorted.
'Someone who'll know how to get you a quickie.
God knows you have enough reason to get a
divorce—Gower hasn't been near you for nearly
two years. I would say he's made his feelings
pretty clear by staying away from you and that he
won't hesitate to agree to a divorce. He's probably
just waiting for you to make the first move.'

'I think it would be best if I go to see him . . .
now that I know where he lives,' she muttered,
picking up the menu again. Sometimes, when she
had first lived with Alun, they had been so short of

money they had eaten only spaghetti dishes. *Primavera* spaghetti, had been one of their favourites; spring vegetables cooked lightly and smothered with a cheese sauce. 'He's notoriously bad at answering letters. His sister said so,' she added.

'He'll answer a letter from a lawyer,' replied Chris assertively.

'I can't be sure of that. He's very free-spirited, unconventional.'

'Mmm, so I've heard,' he remarked, his lips tightening grimly. 'Why did you marry him?' he demanded suddenly, leaning across the table, glaring at her with those pale eyes as if he thought she was lacking in intelligence. 'Was it because your father insisted? Because he found out Gower had seduced you?'

Jessica's blue eyes opened wide in surprise and then she began to laugh, a low gurgle of sound. Laughter changed her completely. It chased the sadness from her eyes and curved her red lips upwards. Her whole face lit up. No longer did she seem a prim and proper businesswoman.

'Oh no, wherever did you get that idea?' she said. Then the laughter faded from her face and she gave him an accusing look. 'You've been listening to gossip about me,' she reproached him. 'I suppose you've heard that I lived with Alun for a while before we were married. Well, it's true I did live in his flat for a few weeks. You see, my father wanted me to marry Arthur Lithgow. He had it all arranged. He was trying at the time to get Arthur to become a director of the company and put some

money into it. I was the bait he used to catch
Arthur, and nothing I said would convince him
that I didn't want to marry Arthur. So I left home.
I came to London, to Alun.' She paused while the
waiter set glasses before them and poured the
wine. 'Alun was the only person I knew who
would understand how I felt. I'd known him for
some years. He's related to the Fairbournes, you
know. He was very kind to me when I came to
London. He found a job for me in the offices of a
publishing company and let me stay at his flat. He
wasn't there most of the time and there was no
need for Daddy to behave in the way he did . . .
like a father in a Victorian melodrama. He came
rampaging up to London, accused Alun of
seducing me.' She took a sip of wine and smiled.
'You should have seen Daddy's face when Alun
told him we were going to be married! He went
red, literally bright red.' She tilted her wine glass
this way and that, watching the liquid slide back
and forth. 'I was more than a little surprised
myself, at Alun,' she murmured.

'But you went through with it. You married him.'

'Yes, I did.'

'And your father forgave you?'

'Not until after he'd had that first heart attack
when Alun and I had been married about a year. I
went to visit him and he asked me then to go back
to work for him in the company. So I did. I used
to commute by tube from London to Uxbridge
and then take the bus to the factory. It was then
that I learned what a financial mess Martin Ltd
was in, almost bankrupt.' She looked at him.

'Chris, are you serious about rescuing the Martins?'

'Of course I am, if only to stop the competition—Lithgows—from taking over. But I want you to be a part of the company still, as an equal partner. I don't want to take over completely, just merge my company with yours. Pollet and Martin Ltd, designers and makers of fine furniture. How does that sound?'

'It sounds very good,' she admitted. 'And I think Daddy would have been pleased to have you as his partner. What a pity you didn't come along sooner before . . . before he died.'

'I did offer, but he wouldn't agree to the equal partnership. He still wanted to rule the roost. No Pollet and Martin Ltd for him,' he replied with a rueful twist to his mouth. He gave her a hard narrowed glance. 'But about Alun Gower who is still your husband? I wouldn't want him turning up now and making claims on you and your share of the company.'

'Oh, he won't,' said Jessica with conviction. 'Alun isn't at all interested in the business. He's an explorer and a writer. He won't interfere, I know he won't. We had an agreement that we should each of us do our own thing.'

Chris didn't say anything because the waiter had come back to take their orders, but he was frowning again heavily and his lower lip was thrust out obstinately. As soon as the waiter had gone he leaned forward again, reaching a hand across to the table to touch hers.

'I'd like to think he would be out of the way,

though, Jess; out of your life for ever,' he said. 'While you're bound to him legally there'll always be the danger of him turning up and making claims on you. I'd like you to be completely free of any relationship with him so that one day I can take my chance with you and ask you to marry me. Promise me you'll write to him or get a lawyer to write to him suggesting a divorce?'

She looked away from him, avoiding the intensity of his gaze. She didn't want to do what he had suggested, but she guessed that if she refused he would begin to argue with her, would begin browbeating her, and that she couldn't bear. Wasn't it enough that she had come up to London with him and had gone to see Margian?

'All right,' she said with a sigh. 'I'll do what you say.' She looked up smiling. 'And now can we talk about something else? You mentioned you're going away on business for a few days? When?'

'Tomorrow, to Germany. But I'll be back for Friday.'

'That's the day the bank is going to foreclose,' she said.

'And the day that you'll have to give me an answer to my offer to merge with Martin's. I'll phone you as soon as I get back on Thursday. Okay?'

She nodded her agreement, but she was thinking: *Three days. He'll be away three whole days. I could go to Wales, see Alun and come back while he's away and he'll be none the wiser. Yes, perhaps that's what I'll do. I'll go to see Alun instead of writing and by Thursday evening I'll know whether he agrees to a divorce or not. I'll know where*

I stand and whether I'll have to agree to Chris's offer of a merger.

When she left the restaurant with Chris an hour later the June evening was still drenched with light as if reluctant to give way to darkness. They drove westwards into the glow of sunset, sitting side by side in Chris's dark blue Rover; past Hyde Park Corner where crowds of people, tempted out by the warm weather, lingered; past the Royal Albert Hall and on past the warm brick buildings of Kensington, on to Hammersmith.

Pale streaks of light still lingered in the sky when at last they reached the red brick detached house on the outskirts of Beechfield, the small Buckinghamshire town renowed for furniture-making for over two hundred years, where Jessica had been born and had lived until she had gone away to London to find Alun and to which she had returned to live when Alun had apparently deserted her; and where she had continued to live after her father's death to keep her widowed mother company.

Chris didn't kiss her when he said goodnight and she didn't encourage him to, but he asked her again to promise to write to Alun and she said again that she would. She got out of the car and it reversed down the drive into the road to turn back the way they had come. Chris lived on the other side of the town not far from his own furniture-making factory and offices.

For a few moments she stood listening to the Rover's engine as it retreated into the distance. The garden, her mother's pride and joy, breathed out into the night the heavy smell of well-manured earth, and the oriental scent of climbing pink roses. High in the sky, above the roof of the house opposite, the house where the Fairbournes had once lived and where she had first met Alun eight years ago when she had been only seventeen, a hazy moon shimmered, its radiance trickling over the leaves of a poplar like a fall of water.

Jessica turned and entered the house. It was quiet and dark. When she reached the second floor landing she was glad to note that no light shone from under the door of her mother's room. Anthea had gone to sleep and so there was no need for Jessica to look in on her and to answer the many questions her mother always bombarded her with when she had been out with Chris.

She went into her own room and closed the door. At one window open at the bottom, the curtains were still drawn back and outside the window the branches of a tree hung black festooned with many leaves until she turned on the lights.

In bed with the lights out she lay on her back staring at the branches silhouetted against the moon-bright sky and tried to compose a letter to Alun. How did you write to someone you'd known for seven years and hadn't seen for two and whom you didn't really know at all? Several times she began it:

'Dear Alun, How are you?', and got no further because memories of Alun kept flitting across her mind, distracting her.

There was Alun as she had first seen him, jean-clad long legs asprawl, curly hair a wild tangle and in need of trimming, eagle-gold eyes glinting with mockery as he had lounged one summer afternoon on the patio at the back of the Fairbournes' house, drinking beer with his cousin Bill Fairbourne, Sally's older brother.

She and Sally had just returned from horse-riding at the exclusive stables a few miles away and had been dressed in jodhpurs, white stocks, black coats and hard black hats.

As soon as she had seen him Sally had shrieked with delight and had flung herself upon him.

'Alun, Alun—oh, where have you been? How long are you going to stay here?'

Skilfully he had extricated himself from Sally's hugging arms and had avoided her kisses while he had answered her questions.

'I've been in Africa getting copy for an article on a wild-life park in Kenya,' he had answered. 'And I'm here just for today.' He had looked past Sally at Jessica. 'Who's your friend?' he had asked with a wicked glint of mockery in his tawny eyes. 'Goldilocks?'

At that time Jessica's hair had been long, almost to her waist. For riding she had had it tied back in a ponytail, but while she had been jumping her horse the ribbon had become untied and the golden silky hair had swirled on her shoulders and had hung close to her cheeks.

'Oh, this is Jessica,' Sally had said carelessly. 'She lives in the house opposite. Jess, this is my favourite cousin, Alun Gower. Remember me telling you about him? He goes to the most fantastic places and writes articles about them which are published by an American geographic magazine.'

'Hello, Jessica.' His voice had softened when he had spoken to her and his glance had lingered caressingly on her hair.

Always shy in the presence of the young men she had often met at the Fairbourne house, mostly friends of Bill's, all of them arrogantly chauvinistic towards Sally and herself, she had merely nodded at him, not knowing that in her well-tailored jodhpurs and jacket with her hair shining on her shoulders she had looked superior and untouchable, her long-lashed blue eyes looking at him down the straight edge of her finely modelled nose.

She had appeared not to be interested in him, but secretly she had been. Dark-haired, his skin browned by the African sun, his topaz-coloured eyes sparkling with intelligence, his lips quirking with sardonic humour whenever he had spoken, he had fascinated her that afternoon.

Two years had gone by before she had seen him again, but in that time she had thought of him often and had even made an effort to find and read some of the articles he had written. But she had never mentioned to Sally or anyone else that she had been interested in him. Her feelings about him had been something she had wanted to keep inviolate, a secret never to be shared with anyone. *Not even with him!*

He had turned up again unexpectedly at the Fairbourne House one afternoon just as she had been coming home from her father's furniture factory where she had been working, learning the business, ever since she had left school. Nineteen years of age, she had lost some of her shyness and had had her hair cut to ear-tip length. Thick and golden, it had curved about her head like a shining cap.

The day had been cold and wet, typical of mid-November and, as she had driven the small car her father had given her into the driveway of the house where she had lived, she had noticed a man wearing a trenchcoat coming away from the Fairbourne house. Immediately she had recognised him. Even now she could remember the way her heart had jerked at the sight of him; the way her whole body had flooded with heat. He had come back, her secret hero. She had been out of the car in a flash and had hurried down the short drive to the road.

'They're all away,' she had called out. 'Mr and Mrs Fairbourne have gone to Birmingham for the weekend to see Sally who's at the university there and Bill has gone to work in Scotland.'

Hands in the pockets of his trenchcoat, he had stared at her across the road and she had wondered if he had remembered who she was. Then he had paced towards her. When he had reached her he had stood in front of her, looking down at her. His face had looked pale and drawn and the golden eyes had been circled with mauve shadows. His lips had been set in a taut line.

'Why did you cut your hair?' he had demanded harshly, and again she had felt that strange jerk of her heart. He had remembered her!

'I wanted a change, and anyway, it was a

nuisance at work,' she had explained. Then, asserting herself, she had added sharply, 'Anyway, what's it to you?'

Some of the glitter had gone out of his eyes and it had seemed to her that he had stepped back from her, not actually because he hadn't moved, but she had sensed a definite withdrawal in him as if he had hidden from her. A faint slightly cynical smile had curved his lips.

'Nothing, of course,' he had replied with a shrug. 'You have every right to cut your hair if you want to. Do you have any idea when the next train to London is?'

'There won't be one until eight-thirty. But you could get a bus to Uxbridge and catch the tube from there.' The need to keep him there, to delay him somehow, had surged through her. 'I expect you're disappointed that there's no one at home,' she had rushed on. 'If you like you could come in,' she had waved a hand in the direction of the house behind her, 'and have a cup of tea and then I could drive you into town to the bus station.'

She had looked up at him invitingly and he had looked down at her coldly. She had thought he would refuse and had been trying to think up some other way of preventing him from going when he had suddenly changed, a smile making two dents in his lean cheeks.

'Thanks, I'd like to come in and have a cup of tea with you. I'm feeling damned cold—I've just come back from Australia and haven't got acclimatised to November in England yet. But I'm afraid I've forgotten your name—your real name,

I mean. In my mind you're always Goldilocks.' His glance had roved over her hair and to her surprise he had raised a hand and had touched it. 'What a pity you've cut it,' he had murmured.

She had let it grow again, of course, just for him. Infatuated she had been, just as Margian had pointed out, blind with a young woman's first love, writing to him at the address he had left with her when he had gone away again, letter after letter, some of which, surprisingly, he had answered.

Shoulder-length her hair had been when, driven to the end of her tether by her father's insistence that she should marry Arthur Lithgow, she had stormed out of the office at Martin's factory over four years ago and had caught the first bus to Uxbridge; flying the coop at last and aiming straight for the one person she had felt understood her, not really sure whether he would be in London or not.

He hadn't been at his flat in Bloomsbury, but the woman who had owned the old house that had been made into small apartments years ago had told her she was sure she had seen him about. So Jessica had waited, sitting on the floor outside his door, because she had had nowhere else to go.

Jessica turned restlessly in the bed, wishing she could stop the flow of memories. Never would she forget the expression on Alun's face when he had found her sitting at his door, half asleep and faint from want of food at one o'clock in the morning. He had been furious.

'What the hell are you doing here?' he had demanded, frowning down at her.

She had struggled to her feet and had leaned against the wall, blinking at him, bewildered by his roughness when she had been expecting tenderness and realising for the first time that she had hardly known him, that he had been older than her, not only in actual years, ten in fact, but also in experience of life.

'Why?' he had rapped.

'I . . . I . . . .' She had tried very hard to stand up to him to find some retort, but for some reason—she knew now that it had been lack of food—she had turned sick and dizzy and for the first and only time in her life she had fainted.

When she had come round she had been lying on a bed and Alun had been sitting on the edge of it staring at her with hard eagle-gold eyes, bright with suspicion.

'What happened?' she had muttered.

'You fainted, or appeared to faint,' he had replied dryly. 'How long had you been out there?' He had jerked his head towards the door of the apartment.

'About . . . six or seven hours,' she had whispered.

'So you've had nothing to eat?'

'No.'

'That will be why you fainted,' he had said, still dry, his lips twisting. 'I'll get you something.'

He had brought her bread and butter and a glass of milk and had sat on the bed watching her eat. When she had finished drinking the milk he had said,

'And now I think it's time you told me what you're doing here.'

'I . . . there was no one else,' she had muttered. 'No one else but you that I could tell. You see, I can't go through with it. I can't do what my father wants me to do—I can't, I can't, so I've left. I walked out of the office this afternoon and came straight here.'

'What can't you do?' he had demanded.

'I can't marry Arthur Lithgow,' she had replied.

'Oh?' His eyebrows had tilted derisively. 'Why not? What's wrong with him?'

'Nothing very much except that he's a widower and nearly twenty years older than I am and I just don't like him enough to marry him. But Dad has it all arranged. If I marry Arthur he'll lend Dad some money to pay off the bank. If I won't marry him then he won't lend the money.'

'You're joking!' Alun had exclaimed.

'No, I'm not. I'm serious.'

'But no father in this day and age can make his daughter marry a man she doesn't want to marry!'

'You don't know my father,' she had muttered. 'He . . . he's very persuasive. He can make you feel like a worm if you don't do what he says. He can make you feel you've let him down badly. And he won't believe that I can't marry Arthur. The only way I could think of to convince him was . . . was to come away this afternoon and not go back. Only . . . only I haven't done it very well. I've no money, I spent what I had with me on getting here and . . . and I've nowhere to stay.' She had trampled on her pride then and had appealed to him. 'Alun, please will you help me? I can't go back—not yet. Not until I've convinced him I mean what I say. I can't marry Arthur!'

Alun had risen from the bed and had wandered away to the window to stare out at the street below. After a while he had came back to look down at her.

'All right, I'll try to help you,' he had replied. 'You can stay here tonight and tomorrow I'll see if I can find you a job. What can you do?'

'I have all the usual secretarial skills and I know a lot about making furniture, the best sort of wood to use and where to get it from, and I've been taking a course in designing furniture and making it at the local polytechnic. I'll soon be a qualified designer.'

'How old are you now?'

'Twenty-one—nearly twenty-two.'

'More than old enough to be taking charge of your own life,' he had drawled. 'So why didn't you leave home years ago?'

'Because Dad made it so difficult. You see, I'm the only one of his children to survive. I had an older brother, Timothy. Dad doted on Tim. The company is Martin and Son Ltd and of course Dad assumed Tim would be in the business with him just as he had been in business with his father. Tim did start working at the factory, but ... but he was killed, in a motor-cycle accident when he was only nineteen. Dad was devastated, and it was from then on that he began to think of me as a substitute for Tim. So I went into the business when I left school too. Not that I minded. I enjoy designing furniture.'

'What about your mother? Hasn't she ever

backed you up against your father?'

'No. She wouldn't. She's very supportive of him and always has been. She works for him too, as his secretary. I couldn't tell her I don't want to marry Arthur. If I did she would argue with me, point out all the advantages of a marriage into the Lithgow family. Arthur is very wealthy.' Jessica had looked around the room. 'Your flat isn't very big,' she had remarked.

'One room, this, a kitchenette and a small bathroom,' he had replied. 'All I can afford to keep up just now.'

'But where will I sleep if this is the only bed?'

'You can have it for tonight. I'll sleep on the sofa,' he had replied.

Jessica shifted again, restlessly, then sat up and switched on the bedside lamp and looked at her clock. Two-thirty—the worst time of the night to be awake and remembering; the time when everything looked at its worst, when thoughts were depressing.

Six weeks she had lived in that small flat of Alun's and she had always slept alone in the bed. He hadn't been there much, as she had told Chris, but he had been there when her father had arrived, informed by the Fairbournes that she was living with Alun.

That was something else she would never forget, the way Alun had listened to her father's accusations, calmly, with a slight smile curving his lips, his eyes glinting with mockery, and when Charles Martin had run out of breath he had said,

'Jessica can't marry Arthur Lithgow because she's going to marry me.'

'Is that true? Is what he says true?' Charles Martin had demanded, and although she had been as surprised as he by what Alun had said she had been alert enough to recognise that she had been given another chance to defy her father's wishes.

'Yes, it's true,' she had replied. 'I love Alun and I'm going to marry him.'

Stunned, her father had left and she had turned to Alun and had asked hesitantly,

'Did you mean what you said just now?'

'Would you like me to have meant it?' he had replied mockingly.

'Yes—oh, yes, I would! I would like to be married to you,' she had whispered sincerely.

'Then I meant it,' he had said, stepping towards her, and taking her in his arms, he had kissed her for the first time since they had met, the way she had always wanted to be kissed, with passion and yet with tenderness too.

So they had been married in the modern way. She hadn't changed her last name and they had agreed that each of them should be free to go and come without hindrance. And it had worked, even after she had returned to work for her father. It had worked until Sally Fairbourne had begun to drop hints about there being another woman in Alun's life; a woman in New York who had worked as an editor for the magazine that published Alun's articles.

'How do you know?' Jessica had demanded,

trying to ignore the stabs of jealousy she had been feeling.

'Because he used to tell us about her, of course,' Sally had retorted. They had been having lunch together in Beechfield High Street at a new fast food restaurant. Sally had just graduated with a degree in languages and had been looking for a job.

'Then you know her name,' Jessica had said.

'Yes. It's Ashley King. Her father was one of the founders of the magazine. Alun is really thick with her. It was she who persuaded the editorial board of the magazine to accept his first article . . . and she's made sure he's had assignments ever since. Why don't you ask him about her next time he comes home?'

The next time had been the following week when after returning from an assignment and being home only one day Alun had announced he had to fly to New York the very next day.

'To see Ashley King?' Jessica had asked as casually as she could, watching him pack clothes in readiness to catch a plane from Heathrow that noon.

'Probably, among others,' he had replied carelessly, but the glance had given her had been sharp. 'They—the editorial board—have asked me to go to the Canadian Arctic this summer, to cover the last part of an expedition that's been following the route taken by Eskimos migrating from the Bering Strait to Baffin Bay. Wallis Grove, who was originally assigned as writer for the trip, was drowned last month. I'll be away until September.'

He had given her another frowning glance. 'How do you know about Ashley? Have I ever mentioned her to you?'

'No. But Sally told me about her last week,' she had replied—and then she had made her big mistake. She had asked him if he had Ashley King were lovers.

If she had wanted to keep Alun she should have held her tongue. After all, she had agreed that their marriage was to be open. She should also have known better than to have engaged in a verbal battle with him. She had been no match for him, and finally, deriding her for being childish and jealously possessive, he had slammed out of the flat on his way to the airport, leaving her question unanswered.

'Alun only married you because your father was so angry with you, you know,' Sally had remarked when Jessica had told her friend nearly a year later that she had come to the conclusion that Alun had left her. She had, at the time, been trying to find out from Sally if she knew of Alun's whereabouts. 'And because your father threatened to sue him for kidnapping and seducing you. Marriage isn't really Alun's line. He likes his freedom too much, and I expect he's been looking for a way out ever since he married you. He's probably staying away from you now so you can get a divorce for desertion. Why don't you?'

'I . . . I . . . oh, because I don't know where he is,' Jessica had mumbled defensively. 'I'd have to see him again before I could do anything like that. Do you know where he is?'

'No.' Sally had shaken her head. 'He's just disappeared. No one in our family has seen him since his father died.'

Leaving the bed, Jessica went over to the window and looked out at the misty moon. She still felt the same about divorcing Alun as she had when she had talked to Sally last year. She couldn't do anything until she saw him first and found out if there was any way of saving their marriage. She would have to go and see him.

'When?' she asked the moon.

'Now,' came the answer from within herself. 'Leave now. You know you're not going to sleep. Pack, write a note for your mother telling her you've gone to see Alun in Wales and that you'll be back on either Wednesday or Thursday. If you leave now you'll be in Dolgellau by the afternoon today. You could go to see him this evening. Go on, do it. You know you're longing to see him.'

It took her only half an hour to pack the clothes she needed for a day and a night, to get dressed and write a note for her mother that she propped up against the toaster in the kitchen, and as she drove along country lanes on her way to M1, the motorway going north, the first pale streaks of dawn were beginning to show in the west. The shortest night of the year was over.

CHAPTER TWO

FEELING the effects of a sleepless night and tired with driving, Jessica did not go as far as Dolgellau that day but decided to stop in Dinas Mawddwy, pronounced *Deenass Mouth-oo-ee*, where she stayed the night in a small hotel and slept a good twelve hours without dreaming in a bedroom tucked under the eaves of a steeply sloping slate roof.

Next morning she woke to a world of grey misty drizzle that hid the hills surrounding the town. Her breakfast was served by the manageress-owner of the hotel, a flame-haired woman, who asked her if she would be staying long in the district.

'We have good fishing and there are many pleasant walks in the hills. And then there's the Meirion Mill. It's open to visitors and you can buy local wool there and see them weaving it into lengths of Welsh tweed,' said the woman, whose name was Eira Thomas. 'You can also take a trip to Bala. You must have heard of Bala Lake—it's the largest natural lake in Wales. You can sail and swim there.'

'It sounds very nice,' Jessica replied politely. 'But I'm going to Dolgellau. Do you know that area at all?'

'Do I know it? I was born and grew up there,' said Eira. 'And my Aunt Bessie still owns the grocery shop there. She lets out rooms too, bed and breakfast, above the shop. You can't miss it. In the main street it is. Tell her you've been staying with me and she's sure to make you comfortable.'

'Thank you,' smiled Jessica. 'Do you know of a house called Whitewalls? It's supposed to be near Dolgellau.'

'Well, fancy you asking about it!' exclaimed Eira, sitting down on the other chair at the table. 'I used to go to Whitewalls often when I was a girl. I was friendly with Margian Gower, see? You may have heard of her. She's an actress in London, now.'

'Yes, I've seen her on the stage—but is it far, the house I mean, from Dolgellau?' persisted Jessica, thinking she would drive right through Dolgellau, visit Alun, say what she had to say and drive right back to Dynass Mawddwy or even to Welshpool that same day.

'About fifteen or twenty kilometres, I'd say,' said Eira. 'But it's off the beaten track, in a valley between the hills. You'd have to drive right through Dolgellau as if you were going to Penmaenpool and then take the second road to the left off that. Not the first road, that goes to Lyn Gwernan, but the second. There's a signpost, but it's small and you might miss it. The lane is very narrow and winding and in bad weather it sometimes gets washed away.' Eira's bright blue eyes gleamed with curiosity. 'But whatever would you be wanting to go to Whitewalls for?' she asked. 'Are you friendly with the Gowers?'

What would she say, I wonder, if I said I'm Alun Gower's wife? thought Jessica.

'I just wanted to see the house where Huw
Gower used to live,' she said out loud. 'I've always
admired his poetry.'

'I could never understand it myself,' said Eira
frankly. 'But then I'm not into literature. And he
wrote a lot of it in Welsh and I can't read or speak
the language. I mean, what's the point? It's dying
out. They teach it in the schools now but they
can't make it the language of the home. And all
the tourists speak English and we make our money
out of them.'

'If you used to visit Whitewalls you must have
met Huw Gower,' said Jessica.

'Many times. He was a nice man, soft-spoken
and kind. A sheep farmer really, for all he wrote
poetry and was crowned bard of Wales. But he
had no control over his children. Both Margian
and Alun ran wild and they both left the valley.'
Eira frowned. 'But come to think of it, Aunt
Bessie was telling me Alun is living at the farm just
now and there's talk that he's going to start an
adventure school—you know, one of those places
where you can spend your summer holidays rock-
climbing or canoeing. Wouldn't do for me. I like
the bright lights when I go on holiday.' Eria
laughed and stood up. 'Well, I must be getting on
with the work. Don't forget now, if you want to
stay in Dolgellau, go to Rowlands the grocer and
Aunt Bessie will see you're all right.'

An hour or so later Jessica drove into
Dolgellau. Sturdy houses built of a dark local
stone glistened in the soft drizzling rain and she
had no difficulty in spotting Rowland's grocery

store that was on the ground floor of a tall, gabled building.

But she didn't stop. She drove straight through the town and out along the road to Penmaenpool. Thin clouds, like grey chiffon scarves, swirled about the hillsides, completely blotting out views of the summits. The surface of the road was wet and slippery and at the sides of it long grasses were starred with daisies and buttercups. Honeysuckle vines twined over stones walls that confined misty green fields.

Jessica passed the end of the road to Llyn Gwernan and began to watch carefully for the second road to the left and a sign pointing to Whitewalls, excitement beating suddenly through her. Soon she would be there. Soon she would see Alun again. What would he say when he saw her?

She bit her lower lip, imagining him making some biting sarcastic remark, and in the next instant stiffened her shoulders and tilted her chin. She mustn't let him intimidate her. She mustn't let him defeat her in verbal battle as he had the last time. She must behave calmly and coolly, and go straight to the point; ask him if he would agree to a divorce.

The car climbed to the crest of a steep hill and through a break in the mist she had a glimpse of the road twisting down towards flatter land, green and cultivated beside a wide river estuary. Rays of pale sunshine slanted from behind ragged clouds, making the surface of the distant grey water gleam yellow. Then the mist swirled in front of the car again, blotting out the view.

A gleam of white on the left caught her attention and she slowed the car. It was a signpost at the end of a narrow road. A Welsh name was painted on the sign in black. Underneath the name were the words: To Whitewalls.

Cautiously Jessica turned the car into the narrow road which was only wide enough to take one vehicle. The surface of the road was unmade and rough with grey stones. On one side a stream foamed white between misty green banks and on the other the hillside sloped upwards, the short green grass scattered with grey rocks and white sheep. The road followed the course of the stream upwards and in parts seemed to be a stream itself because water trickled downward between the stones.

Jessica was just beginning to think it was the original road to nowhere, leading her further and further into the mysterious swirling mist from which she would never return, when the car juddered to a stop. Thinking she had stalled the engine, she turned off the ignition, pulled on the brake and turned on the ignition again. Nothing happened. She glanced at the dials in front of her and gave a sigh of exasperation. Of course—she had run out of petrol. She remembered now thinking that she should stop in Dolgellau to fill up the tank, but she had been so eager to get on to this road to Whitewalls, so keen to get the meeting with Alun over and done with, that she had forgotten. And now she was stuck here, miles from anywhere and unable to see where she was going.

For a while she sat and considered her options.

She could leave the car here and walk on towards the house, hoping that she would find it in the mist. Or she could walk back to the main road and start off towards Dolgellau hoping that a car might come along and give her a lift to the nearest petrol garage where she could pick up a can of petrol and hope that someone would drive her back here.

Eventually she got out of the car and locked the doors. Fine drizzle swept around her, so she took a scarf from her raincoat pocket and tied it over her head. If she went back to the road and tried to get to Dolgellau she would get soaked. It would be better to go on towards Whitewalls. The house couldn't be very far away now and there would be shelter there, and Alun would have petrol, surely. He couldn't possibly live this far out from the nearest town without having a vehicle of some sort.

It wasn't easy walking along that rough road in high-heeled shoes and she wished she'd thought to bring a pair of walking shoes. But then she hadn't intended to do any cross-country walking when she had left home the day before. She had intended just to have a brief meeting with Alun, ask him if he would agree to a divorce and, once she had his answer, to leave.

Sheep, unseen on the misty hillside, bleated mournfully. The stream chuckled over its rocky bed. Behind her Jessica could hear the drone of an engine. A vehicle passing the end of the narrow road? She stopped to listen.

Now, the sound wasn't going away from her, it

was coming towards her. She looked back in the direction she had come. The sound grew louder. A vehicle loomed out of the mist. It wasn't a car but a Land Rover, ideal for that rough road. She waved a hand at it and it stopped beside her. Her heart did a strange little lurch when the nearest door opened and Alun looked down at her, a slight smile curving his lips, his golden eyes gleaming between thick black lashes.

'Is that your car back there?' he asked, speaking to her as if they hadn't been apart for nearly two years.

'Yes. I ran out of petrol,' she replied breathlessly.

'You're on your way to see me, I suppose,' he said. His lean sun-browned face expressed no surprise and his eyes were without expression as he looked her over.

'Yes.' Now that she was actually face to face with him she seemed to have lost the power of speech. She could only stare at him, feeling the old familiar attraction to him pulsing through her.

'Then you'd better get in,' he said, and slid over until he was behind the steering wheel again. 'It's another two and a half kilometres to the farm and you'd find it pretty hard going in those shoes.'

Jessica got into the seat beside him, slammed the door shut and tried to speak calmly and sensibly.

'If you would take me back to Dolgellau to get a can of petrol we could talk on the way,' she said firmly.

His hand on the gear lever ready to push it into first, he slanted her a glance.

'I'd prefer to go home first, have a bath and change my clothes and eat some food before talking,' he replied coolly. 'I've been on the mountain since sunrise, helping to search for two climbers who didn't get back yesterday when they were expected at their lodgings.'

'Which mountain?' she asked as the vehicle lurched forward. She might as well save her breath than ask him again to take her to Dolgellau. They would do what he wanted to do. They always had.

'Cader Idris. If it wasn't for the mist you'd be able to see it, over there.' He jerked his head towards her side of the Land Rover.

'Did you find the climbers?' she asked.

'Yes. One of them had slipped and had hurt her leg, and the other one was sensible enough to stay with her until they were both found. They're on their way to the nearest hospital now, a little wiser and more respectful of the mountain and the weather.'

Hearing the critical rasp in his voice, remembering he had never had time for people who went climbing or camping or exploring without proper preparation, she glanced at him. He was probably thinking critically of her too, because she had come this far without filling up the car's tank first.

'Why did you go to search for the climbers?' she asked.

'I'm a member of the local mountain rescue team.'

'But how did they contact you? Margian said. . . .' She broke off confusedly, realising she had betrayed the fact that she had seen his sister.

'Did Margian tell you where to find me?' he demanded.

'Yes. But I promised I wouldn't tell you she told me, so please don't tell her I gave her away,' she said, turning to him. 'I'd have phoned you, before coming, or even instead of coming, but she said you don't have a phone. That's why I wondered how the mountain rescue people contacted you.'

'We keep in touch by radio,' he replied, and gave her another sidelong glance. 'You could have written instead of coming.'

'I know, but . . . well, it seemed to me I ought to see you first. Alun, why haven't you written to me? Why haven't you been to see me?'

He didn't reply, nor did he glance at her again. The road dipped down into a green valley caught between misty hills and, as if to make them welcome, the clouds split and a gleam of sunlight shone through on the walls of a small white house that was situated on a hillock above the shining waters of a small lake.

Trees, an unclipped hedge and a five-barred gate loomed before them in the sun-shot mist and Alun stopped the Land Rover to get out and open the gate. When he had driven through the opening he got out to close the gate behind him and drove on along a rutted muddy lane towards the house. In the field beside her Jessica noticed a group of stones, some standing upright, other lying horizontally supported by the perpendicular ones, forming a sort of small shelter.

'A stone burial chamber,' said Alun, noticing her glance. 'There are scores of them in North Wales. My father liked to think this one was erected by his ancestors, dark-haired people from

the Continent who came here in the Stone and
Bronze ages, long before the Celts came. His own
burial spot is over there under that old apple tree.
He wanted to be buried near the things he loved;
the house, the lake, the mountain behind.'

Feeling her skin prickle a little, remembering
that Wales was a land of myths, where strange
rituals had been performed long ago Jessica
glanced at the apple tree. Under the spread of its
gnarled branches a white cross gleamed, too far
away for her to read what was written upon it.

The Land Rover lumbered over more mud and
into a yard behind the house. Alun turned off the
engine and opened the door beside him and got
out. Jessica opened the door beside her and looked
down at the mud, biting her lip as she thought of
her elegant leather shoes. They would be ruined if
she stepped into it.

The door was pulled out of her hand and swung
back. Alun eyes, bright with mockery, met her
anxious gaze.

'Are you coming into the house?' he asked. 'Or
are you going to sit out here and wait for me to
come back to you after I've bathed, changed and
eaten?'

'I'd like to come in,' she said. 'But I'm not going
to step into that mud. Couldn't you have parked
somewhere else? Somewhere drier and nearer the
door?'

'No, I couldn't,' he retorted. 'There's no
driveway to the front door and it doesn't open
anyway. Come on, I'll carry you.'

He presented his back to her and she realised he

was going to carry her piggyback. After a moment's hesitation she placed her hands on his shoulders and knelt on the seat.

'Ready?' he asked.

'Yes,' she whispered, and nudged her knees against his waist. His arms came back, his hands slid under her knees and he lifted her on to his back, straightening up as he did. Her hands slipped forward over his shoulder, she linked them under his chin and he stepped forward through the mud towards the porch over the back door.

His hair, still thick and curly, tickled her chin and her nose and she had to control a desire to sneeze. The glints of silver in its silky blackness had increased during the past two years. In fact there was an quite a broad streak of silver twisting back from his brow, she noticed as he set her down just inside the porch door.

He opened the plain black-painted back door of the house and gestured to her to step inside.

'Welcome to Whitewalls, Jess,' he drawled.

'Thank you,' she said, and walked into the kitchen, a big room with a low-beamed ceiling.

'Have you had your dinner yet?' he asked, stepping past her and going over to an electric cooker that was set beside an old fireplace built from blocks of grey granite.

'No, not yet.'

He took the lid off a big saucepan and looked in it.

'I made some lamb stew yesterday. There's a lot left. You could warm it up. And there's plenty of bread and cheese in the pantry. Just help yourself while I go upstairs and get out of these wet clothes.' He gestured to his heavy jeans that he wore tucked into thick climbing socks and began to unzip the lightweight but warm quilted jacket he was wearing over a crew necked sweater.

'Alun . . . I can't stay long,' she began.

On his way to a door which led no doubt into a hallway he turned back to look at her, his eyebrows slanting upwards in a satirical expression that she remembered well.

'A pity,' he remarked softly, his eyes glinting as their glance roved over her, and then he was gone and she heard his climbing boots that he was still wearing clumping on uncarpeted stairs as he made his way up to the floor above.

Jessica sighed and looked around the plain homely room. It looked as if Alun was going to be as enigmatic as ever and she would be lucky if she managed to get any straight answers to her questions and requests.

Very old and rather shabby, was her assessment of the kitchen with its stone-flagged floor, its square table, the surface scrubbed almost white and its dark Welsh dresser pushed against one wall and gleaming with blue and white china. Horses brasses winked against the dark beams and also against the rough stone of the mantelpiece over the hearth, and the chairs were pure Windsor, their seats worn and shiny where many people had sat. The only modern touches were the gleaming electric stove and the stainless steel double sink.

The sink was piled high with dishes. It looked as if Alun hadn't washed up for a month. Taking off her raincoat and scarf, Jessica hung them on a hook behind the back door. Then she took off her suit jacket, pushed up her blouse sleeves and advanced to the sink, her housewifely instincts taking over, unbidden. She couldn't possibly sit down to eat a meal unless she washed up first. Anyway, she doubted if there would be any clean plates on which to dish up the stew if she didn't wash up, she thought wryly.

She turned the taps, but no water came out. Then she realised water was being run upstairs. Alun was taking a bath, so she would have to wait until he had stopped running water. Presumably there wasn't enough pressure in the system to serve both kitchen and bathroom at the same time.

She went over to the stove and inspected the stew. Although pale and cold it looked good, with succulent pieces of pink meat and plenty of vegetables. Jessica turned on a burner to a low setting and placed the pan on it to warm up.

Once the water came through the taps it didn't take her long to wash up and dry the dishes. Then she set the table for two and checked the stew. It was bubbling, so she turned down the heat.

There was no sign of Alun, so she decided to explore the ground floor of the house, going out into the narrow dark hallway. There seemed to be only two rooms at the front. One was obviously the parlour, a stiff-looking place still furnished with big Victorian furniture; a shiny mahogany sideboard that took up the whole of one wall; a neat corner cabinet with a latticed glass door behind which pieces of china and glass winked;

several armchairs, stuffed she guessed with horsehair and covered in dark grey cloth probably woven from horsehair too, their backs decorated with intricately carved wood and a huge sofa covered in printed cotton. There were small carved mahogany occasional tables with curved legs, each one bearing a collection of porcelain figures and china floral arrangements. The whole room was an antique collector's delight and a housekeeper's nightmare, and it looked as if it hadn't been used for years.

The other room across the hall was much more simply furnished. A rough table set in front of the plain window was scattered with papers and at one end there was a very new-looking electric typewriter. A bookcase was crammed with books, many of them looking well used. There were only two chairs, one an ordinary kitchen chair, the other an old ladderback, its straw seat in need of repair. Screwed-up pieces of typing paper lay on the floor just short of the wastepaper basket where they had been thrown. Some snapshots had been pinned to the wall above the bookcase. There was one of Margian, one of Huw Gower with a small dark-haired woman who had presumably been his wife, one of a tall dark-haired woman and surprisingly one of herself taken when she was younger. She was in riding clothes but without her hat. Her hair shone brightly.

The view from the window was almost blotted out by mist, but she could see the land sloping down to the gleam of the lake. It was serene yet mysterious, green yet smoky with mist and grey

rocks. And silent too. Jessica became suddenly
very aware of the silence. There was no movement
in the house, no footsteps on the stairs. Alun
hadn't come down yet.

She looked at her watch and was surprised to
see it was almost two o'clock. If she didn't wake
Alun soon she would have to stay the night in
Dolgellau. She hurried out into the hall and went
to the foot of the stairs.

'Alun, dinner is ready,' she called. 'Please hurry
up. I can't stay much longer—I have to go back
home tomorrow and I have to get petrol for my
car.'

There was no reply, but she didn't wait for one.
She went into the kitchen and turned off the
burner on the stove, then dished up some stew on
to one of the plates she had warmed. Sitting at the
table, she ate stew and bread. By the time she had
finished eating Alun hadn't appeared so she left
the kitchen and climbed the narrow staircase. He
was in a bedroom at the front of the house, lying
on a double bed that had old-fashioned brass ends,
wearing a woollen dressing gown. He was fast
asleep.

'Oh, Alun!' she whispered.

The sight of him sprawled on the bed, sunk in
deep and apparently peaceful slumber, brought
back memories of the time she had lived with him
in the small flat in London. Often when he had
returned from some assignment she had found him
like this, catching up on the sleep he had lost while
he had been away.

Quietly she approached the bed. Yes, he was

really asleep, thick black lashes spread like fans, the line of his mouth relaxed.

Jessica sat down on the edge of the bed and touched his shoulder.

'Alun, please wake up. We have to talk. Oh, please wake up,' she murmured, and shook his shoulder.

He wakened at once, as she knew he would, as he had trained himself to wake, coming alert immediately, opening his eyes and looking right at her.

'Alun, I can't stay much longer,' she said.

'Why not?' he asked.

'I have to go back to work. Since Daddy died Mother and I have been managing the business . . . or at least trying to manage it. . . .' Her voice faded away as she realised he wasn't listening to her. She could tell by the way he was looking at her, the expression in his eyes dark and sultry. Oh, she knew that look. She knew it meant he had one thing on his mind—making love. And the trouble was she could feel the heat of sexual desire flooding through her in answer to it; wanted nothing more than to lie down beside him and lay her hands on his bared chest and feel his hands on her breasts, his lips hot against hers.

She shifted uneasily and started to get to her feet.

'I've had my dinner,' she was saying, when Alun grabbed her, taking hold of her arms with hands that gripped hard, and pulled her down on top of him. 'Alun, no!' She tried to to push away from him.

'I'm glad you've come. I've been needing some comfort,' he whispered as with long hard fingers at her nape he forced her face down to his and kissed her hungrily and mercilessly.

Always when they had made love he had been tender and reverent. But he wasn't now. His kiss blistered her lips and his fingers sought and ripped open her blouse and curved about her breast, pinching and probing until her body arched involuntarily against his in response.

Frantically she tore her lips away from the domination of his.

'No, no!' she cried. 'I don't want to! This isn't why I've come to see you.'

'Isn't it?' he hissed, asserting his superior strength and heaving her off him on to her back, preventing her escape by leaning over her, one leg across both of hers, his hand on her left shoulder. His eyes blazed with yellow fire and there was a cruel twist to his mouth. 'Then you're going to get a bonus, aren't you?' he mocked, and his head dipped down to her breast from which he had stroked away her blouse.

His hair, damp and tangled, filled her nostrils with its scents and her body, untouched for so long, throbbed and tingled, yet still she struggled to escape from the exquisite torment of his visiting lips, his tantalising fingers, rolling away again until she fell off the bed with a thud.

She scrambled to her feet and ran around the end of the bed towards the door.

'I'll see you in the kitchen when you ... when you've come to your senses,' she gasped, and fled as Alun advanced on her again, with long strides his eyes blazing with golden fire in his dark face.

In the kitchen she fastened her blouse with shaking hands then sat down quickly at the table because her legs no longer seemed to want to support her. Hands cooling her hot cheeks, she tried to control the passion that was pulsing through her, searching for escape. She couldn't believe it. She couldn't believe that Alun had behaved in such a way, with a wild wantonness that had excited even while it had frightened her.

She was still sitting at the table when he came into the kitchen fully dressed in clean but faded and patched jeans and a plain white shirt, open at the neck and part-way down the front, its starkness emphasising the darkness of his skin that had been tanned berry-brown by some tropical sun. His hair was brushed but not subdued. Nothing ever subdued those closely-coiled springy curls. Without looking at her he went over to the stove, ladled some stew on to a plate. Sitting opposite to her, he began to eat.

'So here I am, come to my senses,' he drawled with a mocking twist to his lips. 'And I'm wondering what it was that got into me, making a pass like that at you, like I did. After all, you're only my wife. I ought to have had more sense than to expect you to co-operate in something as unimportant as making love.'

The bitterness in his voice seared her, and she flinched and gave him a reproachful glance. But he wasn't looking at her; he was too busy eating. She was conscious of the clock ticking away behind her. Time was going by and she hadn't said what she had come to say.

'I have to go in a few minutes,' she said. 'Alun, we've got to do something. About us. We ... we can't go on living apart the way we have been living.'

'I agree,' he said coolly. 'So what do you suggest?'

'I wondered if ... well, if you would agree to a divorce,' she whispered.

Still he didn't look up. He went on scooping up stew from his plate and the minutes ticked by. When he had finished he pushed the empty plate away from him, drank some water, then folding his arms leaned them on the table in front of him. He looked across at her with eyes as wide and as blank as an eagle's.

'Why?' he asked. 'Why have you come all the way from Buckinghamshire just to ask me that?'

The direct question disconcerted her and she looked away from him.

'Someone had to make the first move,' she said defensively.

'True. A move had to be made by you,' he retorted coldly. 'But for a divorce it could have been made by a lawyer instructed by you. You didn't have to come here.'

'I couldn't be sure you'd answer any letter that was sent to you,' said Jessica, suddenly angry because he seemed to be playing with her. 'It seemed quicker to come and ask you.' She paused, then asked again, 'Alun, why haven't you kept in touch with me? Why haven't you been to see me?'

It was his turn to look away. Lips twisting in a grimace, he looked away to the small window above the sink.

'I thought you didn't want me to,' he said in a low voice. 'Our marriage had served its purpose for you. It had helped you to avoid marriage with a man you dislike, so there was no need for it to continue. I fully expected you to divorce me after you left me.'

'I didn't leave you,' she retorted. 'You left me. You slammed out of the flat in a temper and went to New York to see that woman, Ashley King!'

'I didn't go to see only her,' he retorted, his quick Welsh temper rising and showing itself in the glare of his eyes. 'I went to see the whole editorial board of the magazine.'

'And you didn't come back' she persisted.

'Yes, I did. And you weren't at the flat. You'd moved out, taken all your things with you. That told me more than anything how you felt about being married to me. You'd gone while I'd been away. You weren't there to welcome me back.'

'You must have guessed I hadn't gone far. You must have known I'd gone to my parents' house. Sally would have told you that. Or Bill,' she retorted.

'Sally did,' Alun admitted, his mouth twisting again. 'She told me you didn't want to see me. As it happened, I wasn't able to get down to see you anyway. My father died and I had to come here to bury him.'

Jessica looked around the kitchen, wondering why Sally had told him she didn't want to see him.

She couldn't remember ever having said such a thing to Sally. In fact she was sure she had never said it.

'Have you been here ever since your father died?' she asked.

'Not all the time,' he replied. 'Only since I began writing his biography about ten months ago. It seemed right to do it here where he had lived and where he had been born, surrounded by his books and looking out at the view he loved so much.'

'How is it going?'

'I'm working on the last chapter, tying all the threads together. Then there'll only be the footnotes and index to do.' He pushed away from the table and rose to his feet. 'I think I'll go and do some writing now. I know just what to write next, thought it up when I was on the mountain this morning. . . .' Muttering to himself, he strode towards the door that led into the hallway, and Jessica recognised the signs. He had forgotten her. He'd gone off into that private world of a writer where she could never follow him.

She sprang to her feet and tried following him, tried to drag him back into the real world where she was waiting for an answer, and she caught up with him in the hallway, her hand on his forearm, stopping him.

'Alun, wait! What about us? You haven't said what it is you want?'

He turned to her, eyes flashing angrily, and shook off her hand from his arm.

'Do whatever it is you want. Divorce me if that's what you want,' he snarled. 'God knows you've not been much use as a wife these past two years, so I might as well be without you!'

'Oh, you're not ... not very nice!' she gasped, stepping back from him.

'I never was,' he retorted, and went on into the writing room, slamming the door behind him. Jessica went after him, opening the door and looking in. Already he was sitting at the table putting paper in the typewriter.

'But how am I going to get petrol for my car so that I can leave?' she asked.

'Take the Land Rover, drive in and then drive back,' Alun said coldly, not turning to look at her. 'You can leave it down the lane where your car is when you've finished with it. I can walk down to get it when I want it.' He looked over his shoulder. 'Now get out and leave me in peace,' he muttered between set teeth.

'Oh, I will, I will,' she flared, and turning, she slammed the door to, seeming to make the old house shake.

Seething with anger, she stamped up the stairs to the bedroom to find her shoes and then stamped down again. In the kitchen she pulled on her jacket, slung her raincoat over her shoulders and snatching up her handbag marched out into the yard, forgetful of the mud until she felt it, cold and wet, slithering over the edges of her shoes and into them.

'Oh!' she gasped. 'Oh!' and added as she swung round and shook a raised fist at the porch behind her, 'Beast, pig, mean chauvinistic beast!'

Having relieved herself of some of her anger, she

sloshed through the mud to the Land Rover and got into it. As she had hoped, Alun had left the keys in the ignition.

It took her a while to get used to the vehicle and there was a lot of noisy crashing of gears as she manoeuvred it back and forth, trying to turn it so that she could leave the yard, but at last she was able to swing it round and set off along the rutted driveway towards the five-barred gate that she could hardly see until she was right up to it, so thick was the drizzling mist.

Out of the Land Rover she jumped, opened the gate and drove through the opening, but she didn't stop to get out and go back to close the gate. She wasn't going to get any wetter than she needed, she thought, and drove right on along the stony road.

By the time she could see her car her rage had simmered down, its place taken by a feeling of forlornness. How she wished now she had never come to see Alun. She should have guessed nothing would go as she had expected. But then what had she expected from him?

As always she had romanticised the situation, she thought ruefully as she changed down to a lower gear ready to edge the Land Rover past her car, which had stopped, rather inconsiderately, right in the middle of the narrow road. She had imagined that once Alun had met her again, he would have asked her forgiveness for staying away from her and would have asked her to live with him again. She had hoped that he had suffered as much as she had during the time they had been separated and would have wanted her back immediately. She had actually imagined him kneeling at her feet and pleading with her not to divorce him.

God, what a fool she was! She ground her teeth with rage. Instead of behaving in a civilised fashion Alun had tried to rape her. She forced herself to say the ugly word in her mind, because she hadn't been willing when he had kissed her and fondled her. Oh, no, she hadn't been willing, she insisted, conveniently forgetting how his kisses had aroused her and how she had longed to caress and arouse him. . . .

Something was happening. The Land Rover was sliding sideways. It was tipping over. It had slid off the narrow grassy verge of the road, at least two of its wheels had, and it was tipping over towards the stream, and there was nothing she could do to stop it except turn off the engine quickly. Right over on its right side, it slid, slowly into the stream, and slowly also Jessica slid down the seat, unable to defy the pull of gravity.

Thankful that she had been driving slowly even if her mind hadn't been on what she had been doing, she clawed her way up the seat to the closed door above her and tried to push it open. It took a lot of pushing to open it, and then when it was open came the hard part, keeping it open while she struggled to climb out.

At last she was out, her nylon tights laddered, her narrow suit skirt having developed a split where there hadn't been one before, and, bruised and breathless, she was clambering up the rocky bank of the stream on to the road. Rain drizzled down on to her uncovered head as she stood for a few minutes looking back at the upset Land Rover.

What now? Stagger to the main road, more than four kilometres, she suspected, and hope to get a lift to Dolgellau? Looking like this? She glanced down at her ruined shoes, her torn raincoat. Or stagger back the two kilometres to Whitewalls to tell Alun what had happened to his Land Rover and face his wrath?

She realised suddenly that she hadn't got her handbag—she'd left it in the Land Rover. She looked over at the vehicle again. It was settling nicely into the stream, water rushing through it, she imagined. She couldn't possibly climb back into it to get the bag. If she climbed back in she would never get out again.

So that settled the argument, didn't it? She had no option but to walk back to Whitewalls, because she didn't have any money to buy petrol if she did get to Dolgellau and she didn't have the keys to open her own car and stay the night in it until Alun came to collect the Land Rover.

Sighing, she began to trudge along the narrow road in the direction of Whitewalls. The disaster with the Land Rover would teach her not to lose her temper and go off in a hurry. It would teach her too to keep her mind on what she was doing instead of mulling over what had happened between Alun and herself. But then if he hadn't lost his temper and been so nasty to her she wouldn't have lost hers. Yes, in a way she could blame it all on him. He was so damned unpredictable. Oh, God, why had she ever married him?

She knew very well why. She had been in love with him, and Margian was right, she had seen him as her knight in shining armour rescuing her from a fate worse than death at the hands of Arthur Lithgow, believing him to be in love with her as she had been with him. But he hadn't been. He had only wanted her in one way, to be his bedmate when he returned from his wandering. He hadn't really wanted a wife but a mistress.

On and on she walked stubbornly, her head down, her hands in the pockets of her raincoat. Through the gateway she walked, never thinking to close the gate after her, past the ancient slabs of rock that marked an old tomb, past the white cross under the apple tree which she could see now had the words *In Memory of Huw Gower* printed on it and the dates of his birth and death.

Jessica reached the house and opened the door into the kitchen relieved to get in out of the penetrating drizzle into dryness and warmth. Kicking off her shoes, she went into the hall and opened the door of the writing room and stepped inside. Hearing her, Alun looked round from the typewriter and stared.

'I . . . I had to come back,' muttered Jessica. 'I . . . I'm sorry, but I had an accident with the Land Rover. It . . . it—well, it sort of slid into the stream when I was trying to get past my car. I thought I'd better come back and tell you.'

He continued to stare at her as if she were a

ghost, and then, unpredictable as ever, he leaned back in his chair, put back his head and burst out laughing.

'Oh, it isn't funny!' blurted Jessica, stamping her foot on the bare wooden floor. 'Oh, stop laughing at me, you cruel devil!' Lurching across the room towards him, she began to hit him with her fists anywhere she could until he caught hold of her wrists and held her hands away from him. 'I could have been killed,' she sobbed. 'There's nothing to laugh at—nothing at all!'

'If you could see yourself all wet and bedraggled you'd know why I laughed,' he retorted, his hands tightening their grip as she attempted to free hers to hit at him again.

'Oh, I wish I'd never come here! If I'd remembered how nasty you can be, how . . . how cruel, I wouldn't have come,' she cried. 'Oh, why does nothing ever turn out the way I want it to be? Why? Why?'

'Possibly because you set your sights too high and expect too much of people,' Alun replied coldly. 'Now listen, girl, all this ranting and raving isn't going to do anything for you. You'll have to get out of these wet clothes and have a bath. So up the stairs with you.'

Still holding one of her wrists, he pulled her towards the door, and she had to go with him whether she wanted to or not.

'But . . . but what will I put on when I've had the bath?' she protested. 'All my clothes are in my case and that's locked in my car, and the keys . . . oh, the keys are in my handbag in the Land Rover. Oh, what am I going to do?'

'You're going to do what I tell you,' he replied forcefully, urging her towards the stairs. 'Now go on, go and have a bath. I'll leave something for you to wear outside the bathroom door.'

'Oh, all right.' Jessica gave in suddenly, and after giving him a final angry glare she tramped up the stairs.

CHAPTER THREE

LESS than an hour later, wearing a pair of Alun's pyjamas, made from fine pale grey cotton, and his woollen dressing gown, Jessica sat curled up in an old armchair by the fireplace in the kitchen and sipped the hot whisky toddy that he had made for her. A fire flickered in the hearth, making shadows dance on the walls of the darkening room, and she felt warm, cosseted and pleasantly sleepy.

'I've made up the bed in Margian's room,' said Alun, coming into the kitchen. 'There's a hot water bottle in it. You can go up to bed any time you like.'

'Oh, thank you.' She watched him pour a generous amount of whisky into a glass for himself. In the past hour he had done more for her than he had ever done during the time they had lived together in London. But then they hadn't lived together very much, he had always gone away so much. 'You've been very kind,' she added.

'Make up your mind,' he said jeeringly, giving her a sardonic glance as she sat down in a chair opposite to her. 'It isn't so long since you were accusing me of being nasty and cruel.'

'Well, you are sometimes, nasty and cruel,' she retorted, tossing her head back so that the heavy wave of hair across her brow glittered with golden sparks in the light of the fire.

Alun gave her a derisive glance and then took a long drink of his whisky. Leaning his head back against the high back of the chair he closed his eyes. Across the space that separated them Jessica studied his face, wishing she could know what he was thinking about. Always he had shut her out like this. Never had she plumbed the depths of his thoughts. Never had she come near to knowing the essence of the man. Like Wales, his native country, his mind was a hidden, secretive place.

He would be thirty-five now, she thought, and he looked his age. Handsome in a dark saturnine way, he was thinner than when she had known him and although he seemed healthy enough she sensed a tension in him. There was something bothering him. The book he was writing about his father, perhaps? Was he having difficulty in finishing it?

'Alun, I'm sorry I interrupted you when you were writing,' she said. 'Please don't sit here with me if you'd rather be writing. I'll be all right. I'll go to bed when I've finished this drink.' She laughed a little, 'I'll need to! You've put a lot of whisky in it and I'm beginning to feel quite squiffy!'

'Good,' he murmured.

'What do you mean by good?' she demanded with tipsy belligerency.

'I mean it's good you're feeling more relaxed,' he replied, opening his eyes. He tossed off the rest of his whisky, leaned sideways to put the glass on the table, then with his elbows on his knees, one fist supporting his chin, he leaned towards her.

Firelight flickered across his face and was reflected in his eyes. 'Jess, about what happened upstairs this afternoon,' he began.

'Yes?' She looked down quickly at the mug she was holding, feeling her pulses quicken.

'I'd no idea you had divorce in mind, and having you there, close to me on the bed, excited me,' he said, his voice rasping slightly. 'I wanted you very badly. You've always had that effect on me, ever since I first saw you at the Fairbournes' house, in your riding clothes with your hair all loose on your shoulders. I still want you.'

'Oh.' She flashed him an up-from-under glance. Now the blood was boiling along her veins and pounding in her ears. 'But you said . . . you said . . . that you agreed to a divorce,' she croaked.

'No, I didn't,' he replied coolly. 'You didn't hear properly what I said. You never have. I told you to do whatever you want to do. If you're wanting to divorce me, go ahead and divorce me. That's not the same as saying I agree to a divorce.' He leaned back in his chair again, his face shadowy and enigmatic. 'Why do you want a divorce?' he rapped.

The question confused her, because she wasn't really sure she did want one. Not looking at him, she muttered,

'There . . . there's someone else. He . . . he wants to marry me.'

'I see. And what about you? Do you want to marry him?' He was leaning forward again, looking at her keenly.

'I . . . I'm not sure,' she said evasively, and

lifting the mug drank the rest of her hot toddy, anything to avoid that bright intent stare.

'You're not in love with him, then?'

Lowering the empty mug, Jessica shook her head from side to side negatively, looking at the flames in the fire this time.

'Then why the hell ...' Alun exploded, broke off and sprang to his feet. The rocker rocked violently behind him. He took the mug from her, almost snatching it out of her hand, and she glanced up then, defensively. 'I think that toddy must have gone to your head,' he said dryly. 'You're not making sense.'

'I might have to marry him,' she said. She was having difficulty in focusing on his face, on anything, in fact. Everything seemed a little hazy and kept on changing shape.

'Why?' he demanded.

'To get him to invest in Martin's. You see, we're nearly bankrupt again,' she explained. 'And he says he'll put up the money to save the company. But he won't make any commitment while I'm still married to you. I tried to tell him you wouldn't interfere, but he wouldn't listen. He said I'd have to divorce you ... and then he'll put up the money. He wants us to be equal partners.'

'He wouldn't be Arthur Lithgow, would he?' Alun asked dryly.

'No—oh, no. Wouldn't it be funny if he was?' Jessica found she wanted to giggle. 'You married me so that I wouldn't have to marry him, didn't you?' she muttered, gazing up at him owlishly, 'So it would be funny if I now had to divorce you so I could marry him, wouldn't it?'

'Hilarious,' he remarked sardonically.

'I know now you didn't really want to get married to me,' she went on, rambling a little. 'Margian said so. Marriage isn't your line, she said. No, it wasn't Margian who said that. *She* said I ought not to have married you because you like to be free. *She* said I shouldn't have tried to tie you down. Then who said, "Marriage isn't your line"?' She frowned in an effort to remember. Her head seemed to be stuffed with cotton wool now. 'Oh, I know,' she said triumphantly, smiling up at him. 'It was Sally. She said you were probably looking for a way out of being married to me. That's why you were staying away from me, she said, so I'd divorce you. But I didn't know where you were, so I couldn't.' She stood up to face him and swayed a little, catching hold of the chair back to steady herself. 'What did you put in that hot toddy?' she demanded, her words slurring a little.

'Too much whisky for someone as abstemious as you are, apparently,' replied Alun, grinning at her.

'Oh, now you're laughing at me again,' she moaned. 'You're always making fun of me. I never know where I am with you. Oh, now what are you going to do?' He had scooped her up in his arms.

'I'm going to put you to bed, my tipsy wife,' he murmured laughingly, and as he stepped out into the hallway she felt his lips brush her cheek.

She woke up at sunrise. Haunted in her sleep by the unfamiliar bed, vaguely aware of someone moving beside her, she half opened her eyes and saw apricot-coloured sunlight trickling around the edges of the uncurtained dormer window. She was lying on her back facing the window. She turned her head and saw a lean bare suntanned back, ridged with bone and muscle, curved towards her, topped by a head of curly black hair.

Alun was in bed with her.

Her eyes opened wider and she blinked up at the ceiling, trying to remember how she came to be in that bed in that room. After accusing her of being tight on the whisky toddy he had given her he had brought her up into this room and had laid her in the bed with the brass bed ends.

She had complained.

'But you said you'd made up a bed for me in Margian's room!'

'I lied,' he had replied frankly and briefly. 'Goodnight, and pleasant dreams.'

Before she had been able to make further protest he had left the room, switching off the light and closing the door after him, and she had been left alone in the dark. For a few moments she had lain there thinking that she ought to get up and find Margian's room, but it had seemed too much effort, and then the bed had seemed to whirl around and around, making her feel dizzy and drowsy, so she had curled up on her side and had seemed to slip over the edge of a deep dark precipice and had known nothing more until now.

She turned her head again and looked at Alun.

It was a long time since she had woken up in the
morning and had found him sleeping beside her.
Too long. She had been alone too long: She had
been without a lover for too long. She had been
without him for too long because she hadn't ever
wanted any other lover but him and had been
hoping always that he would come back to her and
claim her as his own, assert his rights as her
husband, while at the same time asking her
forgiveness for leaving her alone for so long and
assuring her that she was the only woman for him;
the only woman he had loved and would ever love.

But it hadn't been quite like that yesterday
afternoon. Being out of the habit of making love,
she had frozen up inside so that when Alun had
touched her she had been shocked and had
behaved like a sheltered prudish virgin, fending
him off as if he had been a rapist, denying him his
rights as her husband after all, but most of all,
denying herself her rights as a wife.

And now, lying beside him, relaxed after a good
night's rest, she wanted him, wanted him so badly
that she was in pain, the desire to be close to him,
to kiss him and touch him, to wind her arms about
him and entwine her legs with his, stabbing
through her.

Without turning on to her side she stretched out
a hand and ran the tip of her forefinger down his
spine, lightly and suggestively, something she had
often done in the past; her way of indicating to
him how she felt. He didn't move, so she repeated
the move, this time spreading her fingers over his
back, enjoying the feel of his warm skin,

luxuriating in the tingling sensations that were flickering through her body and urging her to get closer to him.

At last Alun moved in response to the slow subtle caresses of her hand and he turned on to his back and then on to his side so that he was facing her. His eyes were still closed, lashes thick and black fringing the heavy lids and only the slight mocking slant of his lips indicating that he was awake. He put a hand on her waist. Warm and heavy, it lay there in a proprietary way and then he seemed to go to sleep again.

From under her lashes, glancing sideways and downwards she looked at the dark dishevelled head, the lined high forehead, the devilish slant of black eyebrows, the aquiline nose, the hard mocking lips, the stubborn cleft chin, and felt a new sensation stir within her, a sort of pride because she was licensed to lie there with him, to be close to his naked body and become acquainted with its colour, its beauty and even its defects. She raised a hand and touched his hair. Curls twined around her fingers, trapping them. She lifted her other hand and stroked the slant of his shoulder, letting her fingertips trail delicately and tantalisingly in the hollow of his collarbone before they slid round to his nape.

Slowly the hand at her waist began to move subtly, fingers sliding through a gap in between the fastened buttons of the too-big pyjama jacket she was wearing. One of the buttons popped undone and Alun was able to slide his whole hand through the gap. Gently his fingers stroked the soft smooth skin of her waist until delicious tingles danced along her nerves.

Finding no resistance to their caresses, his fingers grew bolder and slid down under the waistband of the pyjama pants to stroke her stomach and at the same time his lips, hard and hot, burned against her throat, nibbling tormentingly against her tender skin.

Her body, soft and receptive, responded eagerly to the familiar magic of his touch. With a little moan of pleasure she turned on to her side to face him and putting her arms around his neck pressed against him, breast to breast, her parted lips seeking his, her fingers sliding sensuously over his skin, down his back to tantalise interesting hollows.

'Mmm, that's better, much better,' he whispered thickly. 'Now, to get rid of those pyjamas.'

With the pyjamas went the last of her defences, but she didn't care. Desire such as she had never known before scorched through her, melting the last of the frost. And then Alun's lean nakedness was upon her and his thighs were crushing hers and his mouth was feeding greedily upon hers. Her body was changing, growing taut and leaping and twisting beyond her control, offering itself to his in a wild abandon that matched his demands.

Violent and sudden was their union. The culmination of their passion was explosive, a darkness split with brilliant red light. Around her the room seemed to spin and she cried out with the ecstatic pain of fulfilment, and then she was falling, spinning downwards, collapsing like a deflated balloon, laughing and crying all at once while still holding him closely, tightly, as if she would never let him go.

Silently they lay, still close, her head on his shoulder, his hand stroking her hair. Listening to the deep steady throb of his heart, she drifted in a daydream induced by the pleasant aftermath of fulfilment. She imagined that all was right between them, that the past two years of separation had never been. Cosily contented, she believed that they were in the flat they had shared once in London and Alun had just come back from an assignment abroad and there was no need to hurry because the rest of the morning was theirs, to spend in bed if they wanted, lazily making love.

So happy was she, so contented in her daydream, that when he moved away from her, she was resentful and tried to trap him by flinging out an arm. But he had already gone from the bed. Opening her eyes, she saw him, naked, his body gilded by sunlight, walking over to the window. He looked out of it.

The window was open a little at the bottom and through it came the sound of sheep bleating. Muttering an oath, Alun turned from the window and, grabbing his underwear and then his jeans from the chair, pulled them on. Going to the chest of drawers, he took a sweater from a drawer and dragged it over his head.

Impressed by the quick urgency of his movements, Jessica sat up, hunching the bedclothes about her.

'What's the matter?' she asked.

'We've been invaded by sheep,' he replied curtly on his way to the door. About to open it, he looked back at her, frowning, his eyes hard, cold as an eagle's. 'Did you leave the gate open?' he rapped.

'The gate?' she repeated. 'What gate?' She raised an arm that shimmered white and pushed back the deep golden wave of hair from her forehead. His glance followed her movement and the expression in his eyes changed from cold indifference to sultry predacity. He looked, for a moment, as if he might pounce upon her and take her, against her will if necessary. She lowered her arm quickly, covered herself up with the sheet, sheathing herself from his sight, and his expression changed, his eyes became blank and hard again.

'The gate in the fence,' he replied, speaking clearly, saying each word slowly as if he were speaking to someone who didn't have a good grasp of the English language. 'The gate that separates my land from my neighbour's and prevents his sheep from getting in with mine. The only gate between this house and the road. The gate we came through yesterday and that you must have seen me open and close. The gate you must have opened when you left here in the Land Rover. And when you came back.'

'I . . . I didn't know you had any sheep,' Jessica muttered defensively, recognising the signs of his quick temper and hoping to deflect it from herself.

'Did you close the bloody gate?' No longer soft and sibilant with menace, his voice roared, split the silence deafeningly, making her jump.

'I don't remember,' she cried out. 'Oh, I was so wet and tired and my feet were hurting and . . .'

'So you did leave it open.' His voice had dropped now to an accusing whisper and his eyes glared at her. 'You left it open and now Dai Jones's sheep are down there, all mixed up with mine.' His glance raked her. 'God, it's a damned nuisance you are, girl,' he continued, becoming very Welsh in his wrath, 'first running out of petrol, then leaving the gate open, then driving the Land Rover into the stream. Don't you know that there's an unwritten law in the country? All gates must be closed!'

He didn't wait for an answer but strode from the room and she heard him running down the stairs. Blasted out of the delicious languor that their lovemaking had induced Jessica hurried from the bed, dragged his dressing gown on over her nudity and, tying the belt, followed him.

In the kitchen Alun was by the porch, stepping into Wellington boots.

'What will you do?' she asked. 'Can you separate your sheep from the others?'

'Not without help. I don't have a sheepdog. Silverpaws, my father's dog, died soon after he did and I haven't replaced him yet. I'll have to go to Dai's farm and tell him what's happened. He'll come with his dogs and chase his own sheep out.'

'Does he live far away?'

'In the next valley. It's a good walk over the moors and that's the way I'll be going, since you've ditched the Land Rover.' He gave her a glittering scathing glance over his shoulder as he stepped into the porch and opened the yard door. Sunlight slanted in, glinting on the silvery streak in his hair.

'Alun, I'm sorry,' she murmured, following him, not wanting him to leave in anger. The last time he had left in anger she hadn't seen him again for two whole years.

'You're always saying that,' he replied dryly.

'I . . . I'll leave as soon as I can. This afternoon,' she went on hastily. 'I'll get out of your way. I . . . I didn't mean to be a nuisance to you.'

He turned then to look at her, his eyes darkening, their expression brooding.

'You must do as you please, of course. Leave if you have to,' he said slowly. 'That was always our arrangement, wasn't it? That we should both be free to do what we wanted?' And stepping out into the sunlit yard he closed the door after him.

For a few moments Jessica stood in the porch, watching him stride across the yard and climb a narrow path that twisted up the green hill behind the house. She would have given anything to have gone with him, she thought miserably, to walk with him in the early morning sunshine across the moors, to show that she liked being in the countryside as much as he did.

But he hadn't asked her to go with him. He had never asked her to go anywhere with him. Never. Many times she would have liked to have gone with him on one of his assignments to Africa or South America, but he had never asked her. That had been their arrangement, he had just said, that they should both be free to go where they wanted when they wanted. It had been the agreement they had made when they had got married. He would be free to go away for as long as he wished and she would be free to carry on with her life the way she wished.

Sighing, she turned into the kitchen and finding a kettle carried it to the sink to fill it with water for tea. So much for her pleasant fantasy, her self-indulgent daydream that all would come right between them if they made love together. So much for letting herself be deluded into believing that by doing what Alun wanted, by making love with him and satisfying his sexual desires as well as her own, the situation between them would be resolved.

In spite of the ecstasy they had known that morning, in spite of the pleasure they had given each other, nothing had changed, and now Alun was striding away from her over the moors, thinking of her as nothing but a nuisance who could leave if she wanted; who could divorce him if she wanted.

She made tea and ate bread and marmalade sitting at the table, thinking that she was really no further forward than she had been yesterday at this time, when she had left Dinas Mawddwy. In fact she was in a mess, her clothes damp and torn, her shoes destroyed, her car locked up and stranded in the lane and her car keys in her handbag that was in the Land Rover.

She couldn't leave even if she wanted to. She was stuck there until Alun came back from the Jones's farm and did something about the Land Rover, because without car keys and money she

couldn't open her car to get decent clothes to wear
and without money she couldn't pay for petrol to
drive away.

She could, she supposed, try to walk back to the
Land Rover, climb back into it, get her bag and
her keys. Walk there in damp clothes and without
shoes? She glanced up at the clothes rack that
Alun had hung her clothes on and that hung above
the fireplace close to the ceiling.

In a few seconds she had lowered the rack and
was feeling her clothes. They were still very damp
and were likely to remain that way unless she lit
the fire. Her glance swerved to the window and the
sunlit yard. Or hung them on a line outside?

Quickly she took the clothes off the rack and
hauled it back up to the ceiling. Now to find a pair
of boots to wear. There must be some Wellingtons
somewhere. A search of a dark and musty clothes
closet in the corner of the kitchen brought forth an
old pair of boots. They were a size too big, but she
put them on anyway and, heaping her clothes into
a clothes basket she found in the porch, clumped
out into the yard.

The sunshine was warm and the mud was
steaming slightly. The mild air was scented with
the aromas of many wild flowers, grasses and
trees. From the hill behind the house a lark was
ascending, trilling sweetly as it rose straight up to
the hazy blue sky. From a small shed in the yard
some brown hens had appeared and were
marching up the hill to peck amongst the short
grass. Sheep were scattered everywhere.

When Jessica had finished pegging the clothes to

the line she walked around the side of the house to the front. Beyond the small garden the land sloped away to the lake, its waters serene, a cool yellow-glinting blue in the sunlight, dark olive green and deep purple in the shadow of land. On the opposite shore the land rose steeply, lower slopes vividly green giving way to tawny moorland and rising to craggy violet-grey summits.

It was the view so loved by Huw Gower. And by Alun too? Jessica wondered. Was Alun going to stay here, keep sheep and write poetry perhaps, for the rest of his life? Living alone in the land of his forefathers? Had he settled at last? Were the days of roaming over?

She turned into the garden, following the overgrown path to the front door. Her mother would be horrified at the neglect, at the weeds growing everywhere and choking the perennial plants. Lupins had flowered and were over, and marguerites were showing their white, yellow-centred daisy-like faces to the sun. Larkspur and delphiniums were in bud and everywhere was a semi-wild plant, sprays of fine greyish-green leaves hiding a small flower that she recognised as fennel-flower or love-in-a-mist.

She wandered back down the path and stood staring at the calm lake, the distant misty hills. This was where Alun had grown up, where he and Margian had run wild, according to Eira Thomas, because Huw Gower had been unable to control them. But that wasn't how Alun had described his childhood to her.

'My father believes in freedom,' he had told her.

'Complete freedom of the individual to develop in his own way. He disliked institutions. He wanted us, Margian and me, to have freedom to develop as we should, so he didn't send us to school until we were thirteen. He kept us at home and educated us himself—not just reading, writing and arithmetic but how to climb mountains, how to row a boat or paddle a canoe, the names of the trees and the wild flowers, how to look after animals, how to live off the land around us, how to appreciate and respect natural phenomena.'

Later Huw Gower had allowed his two children to attend a co-educational private boarding school where the headmaster had been a friend of his and had run the school on the same principles of freedom of development. From that school Alun had won a scholarship to Cambridge where he had studied Natural Sciences and had taken part in university expeditions to far-off places to study wild life and the effects of climate and geography on people. Margian had gone to the Royal Academy of Dramatic Art.

'But didn't your mother have any say in your education?' Jessica had asked.

'No. She didn't live with us,' Alun had replied.

'Where did she live?' she had persisted.

'Where she wanted to live,' he had replied with an indifferent shrug. 'She believed in freedom too.' And then he had changed the subject.

Was it any wonder, then, given the difference in their upbringing and background, that she and Alun had marital problems? Jessica wondered, as she made her way back to the yard. They had very little in common. She had been the child of devoted and doting parents who had never lived apart from each other and had always worked together. She had grown up in a small town, in a house near other houses inhabited by other middle-class people who had possessed every amenity in their homes. She had gone through the English school system from the age of five until eighteen and had very little knowledge of how to live in the country.

She really had more in common with Chris Pollet than she had with Alun. She and Chris were of the same breed, both of them descended from solid English craftsmen. Both of them had a love of wood, a preference for clean uncluttered lines in the design of furniture and an aim, an aim that had been her father's too, to make available to people with small incomes good well-made furniture; an aim that had brought Martin and Son Ltd close to bankruptcy more than once as the price of wood and labour has escalated over the years.

Yet she couldn't imagine herself married to Chris even if she did divorce Alun. He didn't attract her in the same way that Alun did. He didn't mystify her or challenge her. She couldn't marry him, not even to save Martin and Son Ltd.

There must be some other way to save the small business, she thought, as she stepped into the kitchen again. She glanced at the clock on the wall. Almost twelve-thirty. Chris might be back from his trip to Germany. He might be in his office at his factory. He might even be phoning her

to find out if she would lunch with him and to find
out if she had written to Alun. Her mother would
answer the phone and tell him she had come to
Wales to see Alun and had not yet returned.

Somehow she must get to a phone and call
Chris, explain why she had been delayed so that he
wouldn't jump to conclusions. She must phone her
mother too so that she wouldn't be anxious. She
would walk to Dolgellau even if it meant walking
in these boots.

Hurrying out into the yard again, she felt her
clothes. They were still dampish, but they would
have to do. Unpegging them, she took them
indoors, then searched the kitchen drawers for a
needle and thread with which to sew up the slit in
her skirt. Ten minutes later, she was sitting at the
kitchen table thrusting a rather large rusty darning
needle threaded with darning wool in and out of
the tweed of her skirt when the outer door of the
porch opened and a girlish voice with a Welsh lilt
to it called out,

'Alun? Are you there? Alun, Alun!'

The door from the porch into the kitchen burst
open and a young woman came hurrying in.
Slightly built, she was dressed in shabby riding
breeches, a floppy white silk shirt and a black
riding hat. In one hand she carried a leather riding
crop. When she saw Jessica she pulled up short
and stared at her with wide violet-grey eyes.

'Where's Alun?' she demanded. 'Is he all right?
There's been an accident, hasn't there? I saw the
Land Rover in the stream on its side. He must
have been driving it and that car forced him off

the road. Oh, where is he? He isn't badly hurt, is he? I couldn't bear it if he was hurt!'

'No, he isn't hurt,' replied Jessica, appearing calm as always although she was inwardly very surprised by the way the girl—she couldn't be much more than seventeen or eighteen—had rushed into the house as if she had every right to enter and talked about Alun as if she was a close relative of his.

'Thank God for that!' The girl flopped down on a chair and took off her hat. Her black hair, satin-smooth and parted in the middle, was braided at the back and tied up with a ribbon. 'Then where has he gone?' she demanded autocratically.

'He's gone over to see Dai Jones,' said Jessica coolly, coming to the end of her stitching and breaking off the darning wool. The repair wasn't perfect, but at least the skirt was wearable again. She gave the girl a straight glance and added, 'And now would you mind telling me who you are?'

'I'm Glynis Owen. Who are you, and what are you doing here?' The violet-grey eyes were critical as they flashed over Alun's dressing gown which, being too big for Jessica, tended to sag at the lapels showing too much of her bare breast. 'And why aren't you dressed properly?' she demanded.

'I'm Jessica Martin,' began Jessica, folding one lapel over the other and tightening the belt of the gown, then she added quickly for some reason she couldn't define, using Alun's last name as her own for the first time, 'Jessica Gower.'

'Gower?' The girl seemed to pounce on the name. 'Then you're a relative of Alun's. Are you one of his English cousins?'

'No. I'm his wife,' said Jessica flatly, laying claim to Alun firmly.

'His *wife*?' The violet eyes widened with shock. 'But you can't be that silly bitch!' exclaimed Glynis with offensive directness.

'Mind your language, please,' retorted Jessica, her eyes flashing.

'Well, you are what I said,' said the girl. 'My mother said so. She said you're a silly bitch because you left Alun.'

'I did not,' retorted Jessica. 'Anyway, Alun's and my relationship is no business of yours or your mother's.'

'Oh, yes it is,' returned the girl. 'My mother is a friend of Alun's, see. She went to school with him. My father was a friend of Alun's too, only he was killed three years ago in a climbing accident. Mother now runs a riding school near here, but we don't make much income and Dad didn't leave us any money. Mother and Alun want to do what he and my father had always planned. They want to start an adventure school, and now they can; now that Alun owns this farm. Over a thousand acres, it is, of forest and mountainside. They would have pony-trekking, rock-climbing and canoeing. But Mum says Alun would have to divorce you first. She wouldn't like you turning up, moving in and making demands on Alun or interfering with the running of the school.'

'I don't imagine she would,' remarked Jessica dryly. It sounded as if Mrs Owen had similar ideas to Chris Pollet; amalgamate first and then take over completely.

'And she's going to be awfully put out when I tell her I found you here,' continued Glynis. 'Are you staying long?'

'I'm not sure,' replied Jessica shortly. 'It's been a while since Alun and I were able to live together, and—well, we have a lot of catching up to do.' She managed what she hoped was an enigmatic smile and then, determined to change the subject, she gave Glynis another straight look and asked, 'Did you ride over?'

'Yes, on Dusky, my grey mare.' Glynis had lost some of her adolescent arrogance and was frowning in puzzlement, her black brows making a bar above her violet-coloured eyes. 'You're not a bit like I imagined you to be,' she blurted out suddenly.

'Oh. How did you imagine me?' asked Jessica curiously.

'Older. As old as my mother, who is as old as Alun. Not as pretty. And crabby—yes, definitely as sour as a crab-apple and nagging and whining all the time, you know, like some middle-aged woman are when their husband's don't make love to them any more.'

'Do you ride over often to see Alun?' asked Jessica, refraining from making a sharp retort. There was something about Glynis that reminded her of someone else; another person about the same age who had talked possessively about Alun and had fawned on him like a puppy all the time.

'As often as I can. I've got a crush on him, see, and I came today to find out why he didn't come to see us last evening. He was supposed to. Mum had invited him.' Glynis's eyes glittered with hostility. 'I suppose you prevented him from going to see us,' she accused.

'I would never prevent Alun from doing what he wants to do,' retorted Jessica loftily. 'That has always been our arrangement.'

'Then you'll let him have a divorce so that he and Mum can go into business together?' pounced Glynis, sharp as a tack. 'And so he can marry her?'

'Marry her? Why would he want to marry her?' exclaimed Jessica.

'He'd be better off married to her than to you. She wouldn't leave him, see,' said Glynis, scowling fiercely as she got to her feet. 'I must go. Dusty gets restless and tries to wander back home without me.' At the door she gave Jessica another glinting, malicious glare. 'I hope that when I come to see Alun again you won't be here,' she added rudely.

'I wouldn't count on it,' returned Jessica acidly.

The outer door crashed closed behind Glynis, and picking up her clothes, Jessica left the kitchen to go upstairs to wash and dress.

Sally. Sally Fairbourne. Glynis reminded her of Sally at the same age, she thought. Sally had been possessive about Alun, showing much more affection for him than had been decent in a near-cousin and behaving spitefully and jealously whenever Alun had shown more attention to herself.

Sally, always hinting that Alun hadn't married for love. Sally implying that he was having an affair with another woman, Ashley King. Sally suggesting that she, Jessica, should set Alun free from his marriage because he had only married her to help her when her father had been angry. Sally, pretending to be a friend and all the time slyly destroying her fragile relationship with Alun.

So you trusted her more than Alun because you'd known her longer than you'd known him? Margian had jeered. Jessica bit her lip as she fastened the waistband of her skirt, remembering how readily she had believed Sally. Had she been wrong to believe her? Had she made a big mistake? Had there been nothing between Alun and Ashley King, as he had insisted?

But if she had made a mistake he had made her pay for it by staying away from her, by never getting in touch with her. And during that time there had probably been another woman. She couldn't imagine him remaining celibate as she had done. Another woman. Maybe Mrs Owen, the widow of his friend? Maybe the youthful Glynis? Oh no!

Still frowning, Jessica watched her reflection in the mirror on the wall above the chest of drawers while she brushed her hair with Alun's brush. Behind her she could see the reflection of the bed, the sheets creased and tangled, the pillows still dented where their heads had rested. Memories of how they had made love, hungrily and desperately, the beauty and violence of their coming together after being apart for so long, surged through her mind.

Had their bodies been trying to tell them

something that their minds refused to admit, that their tongues refused to say; that they belonged to each other and should never have been separated?

Flinging down the brush, she sank down on the end of the bed with a groan. Oh, what was she going to do? She had told Alun she would leave this afternoon and he had said she must do as she pleased. She had been nothing but a nuisance to him since she had arrived. She had disrupted his way of life here; a way of life that included visits to a riding school run by the widow of an old friend and visits from that woman's attractive young daughter who had a crush on him.

She became aware that the sheep were bleating again. She went over to the window and looked out. A flock of them was streaming past the garden. Greyish-white woolly creatures, they jostled one another, baaing mournfully in protest as they were urged forward by two sleek black and white Welsh sheepdogs under the control of a stockily-built middle-aged man wearing a tweed suit and a flat cloth cap who was carrying a handsome crook. Dai Jones? she wondered. Then where was Alun?

Downstairs she ran, pulled on the Wellington boots again, went out into the yard, and walked along the side of the house to the front. At the corner of the house she waited, unable to go any further because of the flock of sheep streaming past on their way to the gateway. She couldn't see Alun anywhere.

When the man was on a level with her he stopped, took a pipe from his mouth with the hand that held the crook and, raising his cap, said,

'Good afternoon. You must be Alun's wife, Jessica.'

'Yes, I am. Where is he?'

'He sent a message to you. He phoned from my house to Evans the garage, see, about the Land Rover, and Evans said he would be sending his tow-truck out to be lifting the Land Rover out of the stream, see? Alun has gone to be there when they try to lift it, to see what damage there is to it. I am David Jones and it's pleased I am to be meeting you.' He offered her his right hand.

'Thank you,' said Jessica, shaking his hand. 'I'm pleased to meet you too, Mr Jones, but I'm sorry I left the gate open and put you to all this trouble.' She glanced at the sheep. 'How do you know which are yours?' she asked.

'By the brand on the fleece.' Using his crook deftly, he caught one of the passing ewes around its neck and hauled it towards him and showed her where the letter J had been burned into the fleece. Then he let the animal go to join its fellows. 'Between us, the dogs and I were soon able to separate mine from Alun's which have a G branded on them, for Gower, see?'

Jessica nodded and glanced admiringly at the two dogs that were sliding back and forth behind the flock, on the alert for any sheep that left the flock and wandered off on its own.

'They're very clever and beautiful—the dogs, I mean,' she said. 'Does it take long to train them to fetch the sheep?'

'Fetching the sheep comes naturally to them. They're predators, see? And the secret of training them is to get them young and harness their natural hunting instincts to the service of the shepherd. It's training them so they'll leave the sheep alone that is hardest. If they're not trained they could destroy the flock. It's best to teach them the basic commands before letting them anywhere near the sheep.'

'What commands?' asked Jessica, falling into step beside him as he followed the flock.

'There are only five. Walk. Go on. Go left. Go right. And most important of all is: lie down. That means stop whatever you are doing. Most shepherds can whistle their commands using two fingers between their lips. A good whistle will carry for miles against the wind. Watch Captain now, the dog nearest to us when I whistle to him to move right and catch that yearling that's got ideas of its own.'

Two fingers in his mouth, he produced an ear-piercing whistle and immediately the bigger and older of the two dogs began to prowl through the grass, its belly close to the ground, following the straying sheep.

'I was offered two thousand pounds for Captain by an Australian sheep farmer at the sheepdog trials at Bala last year,' Dai continued in his soft sing-song voice. 'But I wouldn't take it. Captain is worth more to me on the farm than anything else I own and without him I couldn't look after the sheep properly. I would be losing some of them all the time.'

'Alun doesn't have a dog, he says,' murmured Jessica. The sheep had reached the gateway and were pushing through it, urged on by the dogs.

'No, but he will be getting one,' said Dai, stopping to lean on his stick. 'If he stays, that is. There is no knowing what he will be doing yet and I'm thinking he does not know himself what it is he wants to do.' He slanted her a bright inquisitive glance. 'It could be depending on you, Mrs Gower.'

'Oh?' Jessica was immediately defensive. What had Alun been saying about her to this man? 'In what way?'

'It will depending on whether you could live all the time in a remote place like this. Alun's mother couldn't, and that is why she didn't stay. Winters can be harsh. Huw and I lost sheep winter before last on these hills, and last winter Alun and I both shipped our ewe lambs and some older sheep to warmer lowland pastures, and that cost us money. The Department of Agricultural Economics at the University College of Wales has analysed our situation and recommends that the two farms be amalgamated for greater efficiency. Huw wouldn't agree to do that.'

'Why not?'

'He was of the old breed, see? One of the *gwerin*, as we call them in Welsh, tied to his own land that had belonged to his family for hundreds of years as well as to a stubborn culture that produces poets today as it has done over the centuries, living the simple life here and wanting nothing more.'

'And you think that Alun isn't what you said, a

gwerin?' she asked. The sun had gone. Grey clouds were fast covering the sky and already the hills on the other side of the lake were shrouded in mist.

'I know he isn't,' said Dai mysteriously. 'He married you, didn't he? And his mother's blood runs in his veins.' The sheep were all through the gateway now and he swung the gate shut and looked back at her over it. 'Be thinking about it, Mrs Gower. The government offers incentives to farmers like me to amalgamate with another sheep farmer, and once we had amalgamated there would be no need for this gate between our land. I'll say goodbye to you for now. You'd best be going back to the house. It is going to rain again, see?'

The drizzle was wetting Jessica's hair and shoulders by the time she reached the porch. In the kitchen the clock was chiming. It was one o'clock. All the morning had gone by and she was still there, and now rain was sweeping through the valley and mist was clinging to the tops of trees, veiling everything from sight. If she set out on foot for Dolgellau she would soon be soaked to the skin again. It would be best to wait where it was dry; wait for Alun to come back.

CHAPTER FOUR

JESSICA was making something to eat when the back door opened at last and Alun came in. His hair was wet with rain and coiling closely to his head and his thin sweater was sodden. In one hand he held her handbag. He tossed the bag on to the kitchen table and sitting down on a chair began to pull off his boots.

'You're still here, then,' he remarked dryly.

'Well, where else would I be?' she retorted.

'You said you'd be leaving this afternoon.' He glanced at the the clock and back at her, his eyes glinting mockingly. 'It's well past noon now.'

'I couldn't leave until I'd mended my skirt and had found something to put on my feet,' she argued.

'You seem to have done that. But you're still here, Why?'

'Oh, you know damned well why! I couldn't leave until I had my handbag again.' She picked up the bag. 'Is the Land Rover out of the stream?'

'It is, and it's on its way to Dolgellau to be dried out. I couldn't start it because all the electrics were wet. There was damage too to the left side.' He gave her a scowling glance. 'I hope you can pay for it, girl.'

'And what about my car? she asked. 'Did you ask the garage man to put some petrol in it?'

'I did.' He had stood up and was striding towards the doorway leading into the hall.

'Then where is it?'

'Still on the road,' he replied, half turning to look back at her.

'But why didn't you drive it here? Why did you leave it there?' she demanded.

'I couldn't,' he replied coolly. 'You see, I didn't have the keys.' Turning away, he went on through the door, silent-footed.

'But ... but....' Jessica realised she was muttering to herself as she unzipped her handbag. Alun had gone upstairs, presumably to change out of his wet clothes. Delving into her bag, she felt around for her keys and didn't feel them, so she turned the bag upside down and everything it contained fell out on to the table; wallet, comb, make-up, but no ring of keys. Frantically she shook the handbag, not believing it didn't contain anything else. Nothing fell out, so she turned it right way up and looked into it. It was empty.

She was dishing up the Welsh rarebit she had made on to two plates when Alun came back to the kitchen wearing dry clothes, another pair of jeans and a blue denim shirt, his hair rubbed dry.

'That smells good,' he remarked. 'I hope you made enough for two—I'm starving after my efforts of this morning!' He pulled out a chair from the table and sat down. 'Did Dai come for his sheep?'

'Yes, he did,' she said shortly, and put a plate of food in front of him, then sat down opposite to him. 'Alun, where are my car keys?'

'How should I know?' he replied, giving her a bland-eyed glance across the table.

'They're not in my handbag.'

'I realise that. If they'd been in there I would have driven your car here so you could have left ... this afternoon ... wouldn't I? I thought you would know where they are.' He began to eat ravenously.

'I did ... know where they *were*,' she replied. 'I put them in my handbag after I locked the car yesterday afternoon. I know I did.'

'You might imagine you did,' he said.

'Imagine that I did?' she exclaimed. 'I didn't imagine I put them in my handbag—I know I did. I always do when I lock the car.'

Alun looked at her with a sardonic gleam in his eyes.

'You know you did?' he remarked softly. 'Don't you mean you *assume* you did because it's your habit to put them in the handbag?'

'All right, then,' she retorted, becoming ruffled by his calm arguments. 'I assume I put them in my handbag. Now where are they? Where have you put them?'

'I?' He raised his eyebrows in mocking surprise. 'I haven't put them anywhere. I haven't seen them. If I had I would have opened your car and driven it here so that you could leave this afternoon as you said you would. You must have put them somewhere else. In your raincoat pocket, perhaps. Or your suit pocket. Or perhaps you laid them down somewhere in the house. In this room. In the bedroom.'

'They're not in my pockets and I haven't put them down in the house,' she retorted, glowering at him. 'Someone has taken them out of my handbag. Someone must have robbed it while it was in the Land Rover in the stream.'

He gave her another derisive glance but didn't say anything and finished eating his food. Jessica, too irritated to eat any more, pushed her plate aside.

'Now what am I going to do?' she muttered. 'Without the keys how am I going to get into the car for my other clothes and drive it back to Beechfield?'

There was another silence, broken only when Alun, having finished eating, stood up and went over to the sink to get himself a glass of water. Standing up too, Jessica collected up the plates they had used and carried them over to the sink.

'Alun, please give me my keys.'

He drank the water, set the glass down on the draining board and without looking at her or saying anything strode over to the pantry and stepped into it. He came out with an apple and began to eat it as he went over to the chair where he had left his boots and started to pull them on.

'I suggest you stay here until tomorrow,' he drawled without looking at her. 'Until Evans brings the Land Rover back. He might have some ideas on how to open your car and get it started.'

'But ... but I'm supposed to be back by this evening. Mother will be expecting me. Oh, if only you had a phone I could have let her know!'

'Does she know you're with me?' he asked, standing up and walking over to the porch door.

'Yes.'

'Then she won't be worried,' he replied enigmatically as he took down a short waterproof jacket from a hook in the porch and put it on. He slanted her a glance. 'You could, of course, walk into the town and ask Evans to drive you back to your car and unlock it for you,' He glanced past her at the wall-clock. 'Not for one moment do I think he will, though, looking at the time, because by the time you reached his garage he'll be closed, and he isn't keen on working after hours.' He glanced at her again, his eyes narrowed between black lashes glinting with amusement. 'Much better to stay the night here and see what tomorrow brings,' he added, and opened the door into the yard.

'But ... but ... couldn't you, wouldn't you go into the town and ask him to come out?' asked Jessica following him.

'Oh, no.' He shook his head. 'I've done my walking for today. I have other things to do, like feeding the hens and counting the sheep and then finishing that book.' He gave her another glinting glance and sighed exaggeratedly. 'A farmer's work is never done,' he said softly and mockingly and, stepping out into the yard, closed the door after him.

Irritation boiling through her because she was sure Alun was teasing her and that he knew very well where her car keys were, Jessica whirled back into the house, ran through the kitchen into the hall and up the stairs into his bedroom. Snatching up his wet jeans from the floor where he had dropped them, she searched the pockets. All of them were empty. Where then had he put her ring of keys? She was sure he had taken them from her handbag.

Dropping the jeans, she searched the drawers, everywhere she thought he might have hidden them, but didn't find them. She even looked under the bed. Then she went downstairs and into the small study to search the bookshelves, the desk drawers, to lift up papers from the top of the desk and look under them. She didn't find her keys.

Why? she wondered as she went back to the kitchen. Why had he taken her keys and then pretended he hadn't got them? Because he wanted her to stay another night? But if he wanted her to stay why didn't he ask her outright? The answer came to her clearly and simply. He hadn't asked her to stay because he had assumed she would refuse to stay, so he had made it difficult for her to leave.

Puzzled by his behaviour, she began to wash up the few dishes they had used, gazing out of the window at the fine grey drizzle that blotted out the view. If she did what Alun had suggested and set off for the town she would get soaked again. And then it was such a long way, about five miles to the main road and at least another six to the town. It looked as if it would be wiser to stay another night.

The sound of a car's engine made her look out of the window again. A brown and cream estate car lurched into the yard. The door of the vehicle opened and a woman wearing a fawn-coloured, wide-skirted riding mackintosh got out. She had a headscarf over her hair. She slammed the car door and approached the porch. When she heard the knock on the door Jessica wiped her hands on a towel and went to open it.

The woman's wide-set greenish-grey eyes flickered in surprise.

'Oh, I expected to see Alun,' she said. 'Isn't he at home?'

'Yes . . . but. . . .' Jessica glanced in the direction of the hen shed. There was no sign of Alun. She looked back at the woman. 'He said he was going to feed the hens and then have a look at the sheep. Can I give him a message?'

The woman smiled slightly, showing pretty small teeth. Her skin was fine and lightly weathered to a becoming peach colour. Black eyelashes made her eyes seem lighter than they actually were.

'I'm Mavis Owen,' she said. 'My daughter was over earlier. She said something about an accident to the Land Rover, so I came over to see if Alun is all right and if he needed any help.'

And you came to have a good look at me, thought Jessica, noticing how the greenish-grey cat's eyes were looking her over.

'Alun is fine,' she murmured. 'I'm Jessica Gower,' she added, dropping the Martin deliberately.

'Alun was supposed to come and see me yesterday evening to discuss a project we have in mind. Would you mind if I came in and waited for him to come back?' Mavis's smile widened. 'You and I can get to know each other better while waiting for him,' she suggested.

Jessica hesitated. She was longing to slam the porch door in Mavis's face, but she couldn't bring herself to be so rude.

'You can come in if you like, but you might have to wait a long time,' she replied reluctantly. 'I've really no idea when Alun will be back.'

'I'm very patient,' said Mavis, stepping into the porch. 'And I've often waited for Alun. We're old friends, he and I. We went to school together.'

'So your daughter told me,' said Jessica, leading the way into the kitchen. 'She also said that your late husband was a friend of Alun's too.'

'Gareth, my husband, and Alun used to go climbing together,' said Mavis, untying her headscarf and shaking free her shoulder-length dark brown hair. 'It's nice to be in this old house again,' she added, looking around. 'Nothing much has changed, and I still covet that collection of horse brasses.' She gave Jessica another curious glance. 'You haven't been here before, have you?'

'No, I haven't. Would you like a cup of tea while you're waiting?' Jessica asked politely.

'No, thanks.' Mavis sat down where Glynis had sat that morning and looked at Jessica in much the same way that her daughter had, her wide-eyed catlike glance going from the crown of shining golden hair, over the creased blouse and rumpled tweed skirt to the incongruous too-big Wellington boots. Defensively Jessica sat down too, hiding her skirt and boots under the table.

'I have to admit to being surprised that you're

here now,' Mavis said frankly. 'You see, I'd been told that you had left Alun and were separated from him.'

'Did he tell you that?' asked Jessica.

'No.' Mavis frowned slightly. 'But when I asked him about you he just said that you were unable to come and live here with him because you work in your father's furniture business. He said that you and he had always had a very open marriage, allowing each other freedom to lead your own lives and go your own ways and not having to be together always.' Mavis looked up, her eyes very clear, their expression rather critical. 'Hardly a marriage at all, to my way of thinking,' she remarked disapprovingly.

Jessica let that go by. She wasn't going to be drawn into a discussion about her relationship with Alun with this cool cat-like woman, any more than she had with Glynis Owen.

'You said you wanted to discuss a project you and Alun have in mind,' she said. 'May I know what it is?'

'Of course. It's most important that you should know about it. Gareth and Alun used to talk all the time about wanting to start an adventure school here, among the hills. Both of them being expert rock-climbers and canoeists and knowing a lot about survival in the wilderness, they felt they could teach others various skills.'

'You mean it would be a sort of Outward Bound school?' asked Jessica.

'In some ways, yes. But it would also offer some more gentle adventures like pony-trekking. But it was dependent on Alun inheriting this farm and the thousand-odd acres of mountainside, river valley and lakeside that go with it. You see, Huw Gower would have nothing to do with the scheme. He didn't want a lot of foreigners walking over his land, disturbing his sheep, he said.' Mavis's lips twisted wryly. 'He didn't like Gareth. Or me,' she added. 'Unfortunately Gareth was killed before Alun inherited the property, but I don't see why I couldn't take Gareth's place and be Alun's partner in the project. I know about rock-climbing too and I'm a good riding instructor. I've suggested it to Alun several times since he came to live here. Has he mentioned the plan to you?'

'No, he hasn't. When would you like to start the school?'

'Well, I had hoped to start this spring, but I couldn't get Alun to agree. First he said he had to finish the book he's been writing about his father. Then he said . . .' Mavis broke off and frowned. She looked directly at Jessica again. 'I'm not quite sure how to put this, but he seems to feel he would have to be free of his commitment to you before he could go into partnership with me,' she added.

'What did he mean?' exclaimed Jessica in bewilderment. 'What commitment?'

'His marriage to you. He said he thought you wouldn't want him to be involved in a partnership with another woman while he's still married to you.'

'Oh,' said Jessica weakly. This was a different way of telling the same story Glynis had told. In Glynis's story it was Mavis who wouldn't go into partnership with Alun if he remained married to herself. 'Are you sure he said that?'

'Yes, I'm sure,' replied Mavis coolly. Her stare was very steady. Too steady? wondered Jessica. Was it possible Mavis was telling lies?

'I'd like a cup of tea even if you wouldn't,' Jessica said, getting to her feet and going across to the sink, doing anything that would take her away from Mavis's cold catlike stare. 'You know, all this is news to me,' she went on as she filled the kettle with water. 'Do you really believe that being married to me is all that is stopping Alun from going into partnership with you?'

'I know it is,' replied Mavis flatly. 'It's always been his dream to organise an adventure school, and now he owns the land and has the money to do it. Only his foolishly quixotic marriage to you stand in his way.'

'Foolishly quixotic? Whatever do you mean by that?' exclaimed Jessica, turning off the tap and turning to stare at Mavis.

'I mean that he only married you to help you out of a difficult situation,' said Mavis, and this time her glance was more critical as it roved over Jessica. It was downright disparaging. 'I mean, you're hardly the sort of woman to attract him, are you? You're not the outdoors type. You couldn't survive one of those expeditions he goes on for that magazine he writes articles for. You couldn't live in a remote place like this all year around without all modern conveniences.'

'Who told you that he married me only to help me out of a difficult situation?' asked Jessica, putting the kettle on the stove and turning on a burner.

'Margian did—when she was here for her father's funeral. It was then she told me you had left Alun and were living apart from him.'

Margian, of course. How could she have forgotten Margian who had gone to school with Mavis too? thought Jessica wryly, as she turned to face Mavis.

'Margian had never understood Alun's and my relationship,' she said calmly. 'I think you should know that I certainly wouldn't stand in Alun's way if he wants to go into partnership with you. But he'll have to tell me about it himself first. And I'd have to be sure that organising an adventure school on this land in partnership with you is what he really wants to do.'

'It is,' said Mavis with conviction, rising to her feet and putting her headscarf on again. 'Would you let him have a divorce?'

'If he wants one, yes,' whispered Jessica.

'Then I hope you'll tell him that while you're here.' A slight smile played about Mavis's thin lips as she tied the ends of the silky scarf beneath her chin. 'You see, years ago when we were still at school, Alun and I fell in love with each other. Only he went away, to Cambridge, and—well, Gareth was still around, so I married him instead. But we have never forgotten each other, Alun and I, and these past nine months while he's been here, our love ... our friendship has revived.' Mavis raised her head and gave Jessica another cold look. 'If you weren't in the way we could be married, see?'

'Yes, I see,' mumbled Jessica.

'I don't think I'll wait for him after all,' Mavis continued, going towards the porch door. 'Just tell him I came over, will you, please? And tell him also what you told me, that you won't stand in his way. Goodbye.'

The outer door of the porch closed behind Mavis. Jessica stepped over to the sink to lean forward and look out of the window. Mavis stood by her car, her hand on the door handle. She looked around the yard and then up the misty hillside.

If she goes up the hill to look for Alun I'll go after her and drag her back, thought Jessica wildly. She found she was clutching the edge of the sink with writhing fingers and gritting her teeth. Inside was seething with hate of Mavis Owen. She, always placid and usually liking everyone, was actually hating someone! She hadn't known she was capable of such a violent and destructive emotion.

Mavis seemed to think better of going up the hillside and got into the estate car. Within a few seconds it was lurching out of sight. Jessica sagged with relief and turned back to the stove. The kettle was beginning to boil. She turned off the burner and stood for a moment considering what she should do next.

Leave—she must leave, get to Dolgellau somehow and phone her mother. She went over to the chair where she had put her suit jacket and put it on. She was fastening the buttons when the door from the porch opened again, and she turned.

Alun was coming in. He was carrying a basket full of eggs.

'Not a bad yield today,' he remarked casually, putting the basket on the table.

'You've just missed your friend Mavis Owen,' said Jessica curtly.

'Oh? What did she want?'

'To see you . . . and me, I suspect. We talked.'

He flashed her a wary glance, his eyes bright gold under down-slanting black eyebrows.

'About what?'

'She told me about the project you and she have in mind—the adventure school.'

'So she was on about that again, was she?' he drawled, perching on the edge of the table, sitting with his hands under his thighs. 'What did she say about it?'

'She said you couldn't go into partnership with her while you're married to me. Did you say that?'

'Something like that.' He shrugged his shoulders.

'Why? Why did you say that?' she demanded.

'Because I felt you wouldn't like to be involved in such a project,' he replied evasively.

'She said I was in your way,' Jessica continued, 'so I told her that I'd never get in your way if organising an adventure school was what you really wanted to do, and she asked me to tell you that. I . . . I also told her that . . . that if you wanted a divorce, I'd be willing to give you one. Then she left.'

Eyes as cold as yellow marble glittered at her across the room.

'Thank you. Thank you very much,' drawled Alun, his lip curling sardonically. 'Since you and she were so chummy why didn't you leave with her? I'm sure she would have been delighted to give you a lift to Dolgellau. She would also have done her best to open your car for you, get it started so that you could go on your way to Beechfield.'

'Oh.' Jessica put a hand to her mouth. 'I never thought of that.'

'You didn't? You surprise me,' he jeered. 'And you so eager to leave! I assume you haven't found your keys yet?'

'No, I haven't. And I've looked everywhere. Even in your jeans pockets. Even in the drawers in your bedroom,' she retorted. 'I couldn't find them because you took them with you when you went out to feed the hens, didn't you?' she challenged.

'Did I?' he mocked, and sliding off the table he stepped towards her. He raised his arms to shoulder level. 'You can search me, if you want to,' he suggested softly, his eyes glinting wickedly between narrowed black lashes.

'All right, I will.'

Jessica stepped close to him and thrust her hands into the front pockets of his pants, her fingers groping. Both pockets were empty, but her seeking fingers became suddenly aware of the hard bone and taut muscles of his pelvis and stomach through the thin stretched-tight material and were tempted to linger there.

'I hope you know what you're doing,' he taunted, and his breath blew the tendrils of hair that drifted across her brow. 'That's a very sensitive area you're feeling around in. I hope you're prepared to take the consequences of what you're doing.'

Realising what he was implying, she tried to pull her hands out of his pockets, only to find his fingers had curled about her wrists and he was pressing her hands against his body. Protestingly she raised her head. Topaz-dark now, his eyes blazed down into hers, and then his lips covered hers in a ruthless demanding kiss.

Angry as much with herself as with him for letting him trick her into going close to him and unwittingly arousing him, Jessica did all she could to try and break free, without success. Letting go of her wrists, Alun put his arms around her to hold her tightly. Raising a hand to the back of her neck, he held her head still, preventing her from twisting it to break the kiss and his lips parted hers arrogantly to send their erotic messages through to her brain.

Even then she tried to assert mind over matter and to resist the dizzying wave of sensuousness that was flowing through her in response to the familiar scents of his warm hard body and the feel of his hands curving to her shape. But the wave overwhelmed her. Her breasts swelling, she arched against him invitingly and lifting her arms about his neck she returned his kiss ardently, letting reason be swamped by sensuousness.

Slowly his mouth slid away from hers. For a moment longer he held her, his cheek rough with beard stubble pressing hard against her soft one.

Her eyes closed, Jessica clung to him because she was still dizzy with desire, but inevitably her head stopped spinning. Sighing, she opened her eyes and stepped back from him. The fire still smouldered in his eyes and his hands still rested possessively on her waist.

'Why don't you admit you want to stay another night with me?' he whispered.

'No! No, I don't. I can't,' she replied shakily. 'I told you yesterday I didn't come here for . . . for that.'

'Then why did you come at all?' he rasped, the warm glow in his eyes changing to the cold glitter of anger. Grasping her shoulders, he shook her. 'What the hell is the matter with you?' he demanded. 'Why have you come here to torment me?'

'I . . . I just wanted . . . to . . . to see you, just once before . . . before we . . . we split. Alun, please let go of me. You're hurting me!'

'Am I? Don't pretend to be surprised that I am,' he retorted through his teeth. 'God, I don't seem to be able to get through to you with words, so I'm having to resort to touch!' His hands tightened, fingers biting into her flesh, and she gasped. His teeth showed in a sort of snarling smile. 'When I touch you like that it means I'm angry and puzzled, see? But when I touch you like this——' his hands slid down over her back caressingly to her buttocks and he pressed her against him, moving his hips against hers, making her aware of his arousal, 'And like this,' his lips were hot against the tender lobe of her ear and his teeth nipped it, 'this means that I want you. My God, how I want you!' he groaned. 'I want all of you, the gold and shining white of you in my bed, close to me, the gift that was once given to me and that I lost through no fault of my own.'

'It was your fault,' she cried, finding the strength to thrust him from her and fighting to control her reeling senses. 'You didn't love me enough. You didn't really care for me. Not enough to ask me to go away with you. Not enough to invite me to come here. You didn't love me. You wouldn't have had an affair with that woman in New York if you'd loved me . . .'

'I didn't have an affair with Ashley!' he roared at her. His face was pale and his eyes flashed with yellow light. 'How many times do I have to tell you—you imagined it!'

'I didn't. I didn't!' she cried, backing away from him around the table, putting it between himself and her, afraid of his anger. 'Sally told me. Sally said that was why you were always going to New York. You went to see that woman!'

'Sally?' Alun stopped stalking her and stared incredulously. 'Why would Sally tell you something like that?'

'I don't know. But she did.'

'And you believed her. You dared to believe her!' he accused, beginning to advance again. 'You didn't trust me. You talk about me not loving you enough, but what about you?' His voice dropped to a menacing sibilant whisper. 'You didn't love me, or you would never have believed that silly jealous cousin of mine. You'd have stayed on in our flat and waited for me to come back to you as I always had the two years we were together. But you didn't. You didn't love me enough to wait.'

He caught up with her by the door that opened into the porch and bent his head towards her. His breath was hot against her cheek and his eyes blazed into hers again.

'You've never loved me—not really, not truly,' he whispered. 'You only had a crush on me ... like Sally had. Like that girl Glynis has. You weren't grown up enough to love me, you spoilt brat.'

'That's not true!' she flared. 'I loved you—I know I did. But if you'd loved me you wouldn't have stayed away from me for nearly two years. You'd have come to Beechfield or you'd have written to me. You didn't love me, and you don't love me now.'

'Then why do I want you so much?' he retorted, his eyes darkening, growing sultry with desire, his hands sliding along her shoulders to her throat.

'Oh, don't touch me, please don't touch me,' she cried. 'Physical attraction, wanting me, isn't love. It's only lust ... and it doesn't mean anything. It isn't enough—not for me, anyway.'

'You're telling me that this morning ... what we did ... meant nothing to you?' said Alun rather hoarsely.

Immediately his hands dropped to his sides and he stepped back from her. Taking advantage of his sudden sharp withdrawal, intensely aware that she had hurt him in some way and wishing she hadn't, Jessica took down her raincoat from the hook behind the back door where he had hung it the night before and began to pull it on.

'What are you going to do?' he demanded. His arms folded across his chest, he was watching her, his eyes dark under frowning eyebrows.

'I must get to Dolgellau, somehow,' she replied. 'I must phone my mother. Tomorrow is the day the bank is going to foreclose on the loan Daddy borrowed and I promised her I'd be there. I promised her I'd be able to prevent the foreclosure. She'll be in an awful tizzy wondering what's happened to me, why I haven't returned to Beechfield. I'll have to phone Chris Pollet too.'

'Who's he?' asked Alun.

'The man I told you about who said he'll invest in Martin's, save us from going under,' she muttered, turning towards the door and opening it. 'I'll walk to the town, stay the night at the guesthouse there and get someone to see to my car in the morning.' She paused and swung back to face him. 'Unless you'd like to give me my keys,' she said pleadingly. 'Please, Alun. Please understand. I have to go!'

Something flickered in the darkness of his shadowed eyes. It could have been an expression of pain, but it didn't last long enough for her to be sure, and in the next instant his face had hardened and his eyes were blank and cold. Without a word he stepped past her through the open door into the porch. From there he went out into the yard. Jessica stepped into the porch and watched him cross the yard to the hen shed. In a few seconds he came back to her. He dropped the ring of keys into her outstretched hand.

'Thank you,' she murmured, not looking at him, afraid to in case her resolve to leave him weakened.

'Will you come back here when you've done your phoning?' he asked.

'No. I'll drive on as far as I can tonight, Maybe I'll drive all night so I can be at the factory in the morning. I have to go, Alun. I have to try and save Martin's,' she muttered, and turning away from him she hurried out of the yard and towards the gate.

She opened the gate and closed it carefully, gave one last look at the white walls of the house gleaming softly through the mist. Alun hadn't followed her. He wasn't there to wave goodbye. With a little exclamation of distress Jessica turned and began to walk along the lane.

The stream gurgled and splashed its way down the hillside. Raindrops dripped on to her uncovered head. Unseen sheep on the slanting hillside baaed mournfully. Under her feet puddles glittered and stones glistened with moisture.

She walked with a dogged determination through the misty rain, her head down, her hands in the pockets of her raincoat and was surprised when she reached her car sooner than she had expected. It was parked under a tree only about two hundred yards from the gate. Alun had obviously driven it nearly all the way to the farmhouse and then had decided to leave it and pretend that he couldn't drive it because he hadn't found her keys.

Why? Because he had wanted her to stay another night. He had wanted to make love to her. That was all he had ever wanted from her, she thought bitterly as she unlocked the door of the car. She had been his *sleeping* partner. He had never wanted her to be his partner in anything else. He had never wanted her to share his life as a writer. Another woman, Ashley King, had done that. And now he didn't want her to share his life as the part-owner of an adventure school. Mavis Owen, with whom he had once been in love, could do that. So why should he stay married to her?

She slid into the driver's seat and closed the car door. It took a while to start the car because it was damp, but at last the engine spluttered into life and kept on running. Jessica checked the fuel gauge. There was enough petrol to get her to the town and the phone.

As she drove she thought about what she would say to her mother and then to Chris when she eventually got through to them. She would tell them both she had seen Alun and had decided to let him have a divorce. Then Chris would agree to merge with Martin's and save the company from bankruptcy. She didn't want to divorce Alun, but she could see no alternative. Neither he nor she could do what they wanted if they stayed married to each other. He couldn't start his adventure school with Mavis Owen and she couldn't save Martin and Son from bankruptcy and closure. And she had to save Martins somehow, for her dead father's sake, for her mother's sake and for the sake of the people who worked in the small company, the skilled craftsmen who made beautiful furniture.

She found a telephone kiosk in the town and tried her mother's number first, reversing the charges. There was no reply. No one answered the ringing phone at Chris's place either. Wondering what to do next, Jessica left the phone booth, glancing at her watch. Just after six o'clock. She would find a petrol garage, fill the car's tank and drive on to Dinas Mawddwy and phone again from there. Once she got through to Chris and told him that she had seen Alun and had decided that the best course would be to arrange to divorce him Martins would be saved and she would be able to stay the night somewhere and drive on in the morning.

At Dinas Mawddwy she rang Chris's number first. Again there was no answer. She ate a meal at a different hotel from the one she had stayed in before, not wanting to meet the curious Eira again. She took her time about eating and it was going on for quarter to nine when she tried again to reach Chris and then her mother and failed again, neither of them being at home, so she decided to drive on through the night to reach Beechfield by morning.

It was when she was on the M1 with only a few miles to go to the exit road she would take for Aylesbury and Beechfield and dawn was streaking the sky in the east that the tedium of driving along the straight dull road had its effect. She went to sleep at the wheel. The car swerved off the road, and somersaulted into a ditch. Jessica was very badly injured, and it was a long time before she recovered sufficiently to remember where she had been and where she had been going when the accident happened.

CHAPTER FIVE

She opened her eyes and looked around the room. It was a small room, very plain. The walls were painted a pleasant soft pink and the trim around the window and the double swing doors was white. She was lying in a high narrow bed covered in hygienic white. A tube attached to a bottle half full of a colourless liquid that was strung above her disappeared under the wide sleeve of the white gown she was wearing. The tube seemed to be attached to her left arm. There was a locker beside the bed. On it was a vase of flowers and a water-jug and a glass. On the wall opposite to her hung a television set. Through the window she could see the tops of trees waving in a wind. The sky behind the trees was grey and cloudy.

Puzzled, she tried to sit up and failed. She tried to move her legs and also failed. Panic flickered through her, and she called out.

'Help! Help me!' Her voice was weak, creaking as if it hadn't been used much lately. Its weakness increased her panic. She was in a strange place, her head felt as if it was stuffed with cottonwool and she had no idea who she was or how she had come there. She tried again to shout. The noise she made was louder. One of the swing doors was already open, and a woman appeared in the opening. She was dressed in a nurse's uniform and was carrying a small tray. She walked over to the bed. Her cheeks were shiny and red and her eyes smiled.

'What is this place?' asked Jessica.

'The County Hospital,' replied the nurse, putting the small tray on the locker.

'What am I doing here?' asked Jessica next.

'Getting better, I hope,' replied the nurse, smiling. 'It's nice to hear you talking. You've been silent an awful long time.'

'How long have I been here?'

'Over six weeks.'

'Oh.' Jessica frowned. It seemed now that her brain was filled with grey stuff that blotted out everything. It was like being in a thick fog. 'Why?' she muttered. 'I don't seem to be able to remember anything. Do you know . . . I mean, would you tell me who I am?'

'Oh, my God!' exclaimed the nurse, and hurried from the room.

When she came back there was another nurse with her, an older woman in a slightly different uniform, whose lean long face was marked by the severe lines of authority. Her eyes were a cold bluish-grey and their glance was sharp.

'How are you feeling today?' she asked.

'I'm not sure. I don't seem to be able to move and I don't know who I am.' Tears of weakness welled in Jessica's eyes. 'Please will you tell me my name?'

'You're Jessica Martin,' replied the older nurse. The younger one hovered behind her, her brown eyes wide with curiosity. 'You were in a very bad car accident. It happened when you were returning home from Wales, I believe. You've been in a coma for some time, but this week, we're glad to say, you've shown signs of consciousness. We're very pleased, and as soon as we can we'll take you off intravenous and other life-support systems and you'll be able to feed yourself and have physiotherapy exercises to strengthen your muscles so you can walk again.'

'Thank you.' Jessica was silent for a few moments as she absorbed all that the nurse had told her and tried to make sense of it. She had recognised her name and memories were beginning to flicker through her mind; memories of her mother and father, of her home in Beechfield.

'I'm Sister Leyland,' continued the older nurse, 'and this is Staff Nurse Blewitt. We've been looking after you in this intensive care unit while you were in the coma.' She stared intently at Jessica. 'Do you remember anything now?'

'Some things. I remember my parents and my home in Beechfield. Where exactly is this hospital?'

'Near Aylesbury. You were brought straight here after the accident.'

'I don't remember anything about the accident or what happened before. I wonder what I'd been doing in Wales?' muttered Jessica.

'Well, don't worry about that now. As you get stronger I'm sure you'll remember more,' said Sister Leyland practically. 'Your mother will be here soon to visit you and you'll be able to ask her more. Maybe the sight of her will trigger off your memory. Let's hope so.'

After her temperature had been taken Jessica lay

quietly watching the trees through the window, making herself go over what the nurse had told her, afraid she might forget it. Wales. Where was Wales? Well, that part of her memory was working all right. She knew where Wales was. It was to the west of England, a beautiful country, a place of mountains, glens and lakes, all shrouded mysteriously in mist.

What had she been doing there? Desperately she tried to remember, but like the mountains of Wales her mind was also shrouded in grey mist and trying to see through the mist made her head ache. She felt very tired so she closed her eyes and slept.

When she opened her eyes again a woman was standing beside the locker arranging some long-stemmed pink roses in a vase. She was a tallish woman with fair greying hair cut short and she was wearing a suit of blue tweed with a white frilly blouse. When she had finished arranging the flowers she stood back to admire them. She caught sight of Jessica looking up at her and smiled, showing perfect teeth, her grey eyes glinting with affection and good humour.

'Hello, darling,' she said, sitting down on a chair beside the bed. 'Did you have a nice sleep?'

'Yes, thanks.' Jessica smiled too and lifted one of her hands from the bed and held it out rather weakly. 'Hello, Mother,' she murmured.

'It's so good to hear you speaking at last,' replied Anthea Martin, taking Jessica's thin hand in both of hers. Tears shone in her grey eyes. 'It's been such a long time since the accident. You've been so ill. There were times when ... when I thought you would never get better; that you'd be on those life-supporting machines for the rest of your life. But the surgeons and the nurses have been marvellous, and today they tell me you've really turned the corner and it won't be long before you're walking again and you'll be able to come home.'

'I can't remember,' whispered Jessica. 'I can't remember much about myself before I woke up and found myself here this afternoon. I couldn't remember who I was. They had to tell me.'

'Oh, my poor darling!' Anthea looked very concerned. 'How awful for you. But you remember me, don't you?'

'Yes, I do. I remember you and Dad ... and I think I remember the house. But everything else is blotted out by fog. There's a fog in my mind and I can't see through it. It's like the mist was.'

'What mist, darling?'

'The mist on the hills.' Jessica closed her eyes and immediately she was in a garden in front of a house with white walls. The garden was full of flowers. She opened her eyes and smiled at her mother. 'You would have liked the garden,' she said, 'but it needed weeding.'

'What garden?' asked Anthea, looking puzzled.

'I don't know—I can't remember.' Jessica frowned. Her head ached. 'I can't remember anything,' she moaned. 'Oh, what am I going to do? The nurse said I was in an accident and it happened near here.'

'That's right—on the M1. You went off the

road. The police think you might have gone to sleep at the wheel. It happened early in the morning. You suffered injuries to your head, ribs and spine and you were in a coma until just this week. We've all been very worried about you.' Anthea's voice choked a little and taking a handkerchief from her handbag she blew her nose and wiped her eyes. Then she attempted a smile. 'But now you're going to get better, and when you're stronger and you're able to move about I'm sure your memory will return.'

But what Anthea Martin hoped would happen didn't happen. Although Jessica did get stronger and was taken off intravenous feeding and was able to begin the physiotherapy the fog remained in her mind, shrouding from her everything she had done or had happened to her during the two years preceding the accident. She knew who she was. She knew she was married. She knew she had worked in her father's furniture company, but she remembered nothing of the time that had passed since Alun had returned from an assignment in South America two years ago. She remembered nothing of their quarrel, their separation and their meeting again in Wales.

Several times she was visited by a doctor of psychiatry, a small Indian woman called Dr Mehta, who sat with her and talked about the problem of loss of memory.

'Often it happens when a person suffers a great shock to the system, as you have,' she explained. 'You are experiencing a mental black-out which is acting as a sort of protection. It's possible that there are happenings in your life that you don't want to remember; problems that caused you distress and pain. But I don't want you to force yourself to remember. Just take each day as it comes and concentrate on building up your health and strength. We'll talk about what you do remember every day and perhaps gradually you'll start to remember more.'

Strength returned to Jessica's muscles very slowly. At last she was able to sit up without support and to feed herself. Then came the trips to the physiotherapy department, in a wheelchair. The days went by. Outside the window of her room the leaves on the trees began to change colour as September gave way to October. Anthea visited her every day.

'They tell me you were able to take a few steps by yourself today,' Anthea said one wet and windy afternoon. 'How's the old memory? Have you remembered yet why you went to Wales.'

'No. I don't remember anything about Wales.'

'Do you remember working at the furniture factory?' asked Anthea casually. She was busy arranging flowers again—chrysanthemums this time, big shaggy golden-brown blooms that she had grown herself.

'Vaguely. Mother, was there some sort of problem connected with the company? I seem to remember being worried about the company and planning to do something to save it.'

Anthea gave her a sharp glance.

'Yes, there was a problem. But I'm not going to tell you what it was because Dr Mehta says I mustn't tell you too much. It's best if you remember by yourself. I'll just tell you that the problem was solved and you have nothing to worry about. I sold out to Lithgows. They own the company now. It's what your father would have wanted.'

The mists in Jessica's mind swirled and lifted a little. The name Lithgow meant something to her. She remembered a man called Arthur Lithgow.

'Arthur,' she whispered. 'Arthur Lithgow. I remember him. Dad wanted me to marry him.'

'Wonderful!' beamed Anthea. 'You've remembered something else! It was the name, wasn't it? The name shone through the mist in your mind.'

'But why did you sell out to him? There was someone else wasn't there? I'm sure there was someone else who was interested in helping us; something else we could have done.'

'Listen to me,' said Anthea authoritatively. 'When you didn't return from Wales, and then when the police came and told me you'd been seriously injured and were in a coma, I had to act on my own. The bank would have foreclosed if I hadn't and Martin and Son Ltd would have been lost. So I went to Arthur and he agreed to take over the company and to continue to employ myself and you.'

'But . . . but . . .' Jessica struggled to hold back the mist, but it came down, blotting out everything. 'Oh, it's no use—I can't remember what I was going to do; why I was driving back to

Beechfield. I didn't want to come back. I didn't want to leave Wales. But I had to come back to save Martins. I'm sure there was something I was going to do. Oh, Mother what's going to happen to me? I can't walk properly and I can't remember. I'm useless. . . .'

She broke down then and two nurses hurried into the room. For a while everything was confused and they told her later that she had had a relapse. For a while there were no exercises, no visits from Dr Mehta, only rest and drug-induced sleep until she was tranquil again. By the time she had recovered the few leaves clinging to the branches of the trees she could see were brown and withered, and in the next few days they were blown away. November had come.

The physiotherapy exercises were started again, but she made no attempt to walk, seeming to be content to sit in her wheelchair and read mystery novels. One day when Anthea visited her, she brought roses; red roses still in bud, misted by a delicate fronds of maidenhair; a bouquet arranged by a skilled florist. There was a card with them, and Jessica took it out of its envelope. The message written on it was simple. *See you soon, Alun.*

She stared at the name. Alun. The mists swirled in her mind and lifted a little. Into a bright clearing swam the image of a man's face, lean and dark-browed with a mockingly slanted mouth and eagle-gold eyes. Alun, her husband. She looked up at Anthea.

'Where is Alun now?' she asked.

'Still in Wales, dear, but coming to see you as soon as he can,' replied Anthea, watching closely.

Jessica looked down at the roses that were lying across her lap. She touched one of them with a fingertip.

'I went to Wales to see him,' she murmured. 'But I can't remember why I went.' She looked up at her mother again. 'Do you know why I went?'

'No, dear, I don't. You just decided to go—left me a note to say where you'd gone and when you'd be back.'

'Does he know I was in an accident?'

For a moment Anthea looked acutely uncomfortable as if she had been caught out doing something she shouldn't.

'He knows now. I . . . I wrote to him telling him when you had that relapse. These flowers and a letter to me from him arrived today. He'll be here tomorrow.'

The mists swirled again, thickening. Jessica stared at the name written on the card again hoping it would trigger off more memories of Alun, but nothing happened.

Yet she recognised him as soon as he stepped into her room the next day and felt her heart leap in her breast with excitement. Dressed in a suit made from beige corduroy and a cream-coloured shirt, he looked dark and intense. He approached her warily and then went down suddenly on his knees beside her chair.

'Jess—oh, Jess, I'm so sorry,' he murmured, and kissed her cheek. 'I didn't know you'd been hurt.

All these months, and I didn't know until last week. I wasn't told. Why wasn't I told?'

'I don't know,' she whispered, holding his hands and gazing at him. 'But I'm glad you've come. I've been longing for you to come. Please kiss me again.'

He bent his head and kissed her offered lips. Closing her eyes, she let the warm comfort of the sweet caress flow through her. When it was over he stood up and brought a chair over so he could sit close beside her.

'Have they ... I mean, has Mother told you I have some sort of amnesia and I can't remember much about my life before the accident?' asked Jessica. 'I can't remember why I went to Wales. Mother told me I went to visit you. Was she right?'

'Yes. But you remembered me when I came in just now. You remember that we're married to each other?'

'Oh yes, I remember that. I remember most of my life before the accident,' she said, smiling at him. 'About us getting married and living in the flat together. What were you doing in Wales?'

'Writing a book about my father. I've finished it now and it's with the publisher.' Alun's eyes narrowed he studied her closely. 'You don't remember anything about coming to see me there?'

'Nothing.' She shook her head and her hair, which had grown thick and long, shimmered in the light from the window. She looked right at him, her eyes clear and wide. 'I can't remember anything since the last time I saw you.'

'And when was that?' He was frowning now, dark eyebrows slanting downwards.

'At the flat. You'd just come back from an assignment I think you'd been to South America again.' Her brow wrinkled as she struggled to remember. 'I remember being glad you were back and were safe. I think I didn't want you to go away again, but . . .' She broke off, shaking her head again. 'I . . . I can't remember any more, and it makes me very tired trying to see through the fog in my mind.' She looked at him appealingly, turning to him for help as she always had done. 'Oh, Alun, what am I going to do? I can't remember part of my life. I can't remember two whole years of it.'

'Perhaps that part wasn't worth remembering,' he pointed out, holding both her hands in his. 'Perhaps it's best forgotten. Don't try so hard to remember. Let it be. Concentrate on getting well enough to leave this place. I want you out of here as soon as possible to take you away with me. We'll go far away to a place I know where I can look after you. We'll have a holiday together.'

'But . . . but . . . they won't let me leave here until . . . until I can walk properly,' she replied, gazing at him adoringly. He was back, her knight errant who had always come to her aid, who had always helped her when she had had a problem.

'They will when they know I'm going to take care of you. They've already told me they can't do much more for you. Physically you're healthy. It's just something mental that's preventing you from walking and from remembering.' Alun paused and gave her a wary glance. 'You would like to go away with me, wouldn't you? You always used to say you would.'

'Oh, yes. I'd love to go away with you. But where? Where will we go?' She felt again the sudden excited leap of her heart.

'You'll see when we get there,' he said teasingly, and rose to his feet. She felt panic streak through her. He was going, leaving her, and she felt she couldn't bear the pain of parting from him. She reached out, grasped his nearest hand and clung to it.

'Don't go,' she pleaded.

'I must. Visiting time is over.'

'But you'll come again? Tomorrow?'

'You want me to come?'

'Yes, yes, I do. Please come every day . . . until I can leave with you.'

'I'll do my best,' he promised, and bending, kissed her again, lightly on the lips. When she opened her eyes after the kiss had ended he had gone.

After he had gone she sat quietly for a long time thinking about him. Strange that she could remember meeting him and falling in love with him and marrying him quite vividly, but whenever she tried to get beyond his return from South America she came up against thick fog.

Next day at her session with Dr Mehta she told the psychiatrist what had happened when she had seen Alun the day before, how she had remembered him immediately and how she remembered the first two years of the marriage. The psychiatrist listened as she always did with her sleek dark head tilted slightly to one side, her large brown eyes soft with compassion.

'Something must have happened at that point that you didn't like,' she said after a while. 'Something that hurt you, and now your mind is refusing to face up to that painful reality. How did your husband react to your amnesia?'

'He told me not to try so hard to remember, to let it be.'

'That was good advice. Is he coming to see you?'

'Yes, he is. He wants to take me away on holiday with him, if the hospital will release me.'

'He won't have any trouble in getting the authorities here to do that. We've done all we can to help you, and since he has shown a desire to look after you I think we can let him take over your rehabilitation. But I must have a few words with him about your loss of memory. It's important that he doesn't tell you anything of the happenings during the past two years of your life and your visit to Wales. You must be given every opportunity to remember what happened naturally. Only in that way will you be sure that your memory has really returned to normal and further shock can be avoided. Do you understand?'

'Yes, I think so.'

'As the days go by and you see your husband more often it's possible you'll remember more and more. It was a good idea of your mother's to send for him.' Dr Mehta stood up. 'I'll see you again, the day after tomorrow if nothing happens before then to make it necessary for me to talk with you.'

The doctor left the room, and Jessica sat as if turned to stone staring out at the wind-tossed bare branches of the trees. Her mother had sent for Alun; he hadn't come of his own accord. Why not?

She was restless all that night, thinking about Alun, wondering why he hadn't come to visit her sooner. Questions about their relationship tormented her and remained unanswered because her mind refused to find the anwers. They were there somewhere in the mist that shrouded her memory. Determined to ask him about the state of their marriage, she felt frustrated when he didn't come to see her the next day, and when her mother arrived at visiting time, instead of greeting Anthea with pleasure as she usually did she demanded irritably,

'Where's Alun?'

'He had to go up to London to see an editor at the publishing company that's publishing the book about his father. He sent his love to you and said he'll see you tomorrow for sure.' Anthea settled into her chair. 'It was my idea to send for him, you know,' she continued. 'I felt sure you'd begin to get better as soon as you saw him. You're looking much brighter today—more like yourself, not so vague and listless.'

'But I still can't remember why I went to Wales to see him and what happened there,' grumbled Jessica. 'Why hasn't he visited me before? Why didn't he know I'd been in an accident? Why didn't you tell him? Why didn't the police tell him instead of telling you?'

'Well, they told me first because the address of

the Beechfield house was on your driver's licence
and they assumed quite rightly that you lived
there,' replied Anthea evasively. 'You had nothing
on you that indicated that you're Alun's wife. You
didn't change your last name when you married,
you know.' Anthea looked disapproving.

'Oh, didn't I?' That was something she hadn't
remembered. 'Why not?'

'Because it's the fashion nowadays for a woman
to keep her last name when she marries, especially
if she has a career she wishes to continue,' replied
Anthea coolly. 'I can't say I think much of these
new-fangled ideas about marriage, this being
married but living apart business that you and
Alun have always gone in for ...' She broke off
suddenly with a gasp, her hand going to her
mouth. 'Oh, dear,' she muttered, 'now I've done it!
Dr Mehta said I wasn't to mention anything to
you that you couldn't remember yourself.' She
looked worriedly at Jessica. 'I didn't tell Alun
you'd been in an accident at first because I wasn't
sure, you see, how things were between you and
him. Your relationship seemed so strange to me,'
she added with a sigh. 'When I did tell him he
wrote back to say that as long as I kept in touch
with him and kept him informed about your
progess he would stay at the farm to attend to
some business he had to do in Wales.'

'I see.' Jessica felt suddenly miserable. His
business had meant more to Alun than she had.
'So we weren't living together when I went to see
him in Wales.'

'No, you weren't.'

'Why not?'

'I really can't answer that, darling,' said Anthea. 'You and he have your own arrangement. You always have had. Freedom to come and go as you both please—very necessary when you're married to a free-spirit like Alun, you once told me, although I'm not sure what you meant. Freedom for me came when I married your father, and at last I was able to do the things I'd always wanted to do. His love and support freed my spirit. But I don't expect you understand that.' She rose to her feet. 'I can't stay any longer. Alun will be here again tomorrow. He's taken over the care of you, thank goodness. He's really turned out to be a much more reliable and sensible person than I had ever thought him to be—quite responsible and mature. And he's going to take you away on holiday for a while.' Anthea smiled. 'And that's the best thing that could happen to both of you, and it proves how much he cares for you and how much he wants you to get better.'

'Yes, I suppose it does,' said Jessica, but she didn't feel at all assured that all was well between her and Alun.

Next day when he visited her she refrained from asking him questions about their marriage, sensing instinctively that she might find the truth painful. While she couldn't remember what had happened during the past two years she could pretend that their marriage had been happy and normal. Yet during the next and last week of her stay in hospital she became more and more convinced that Alun was only visiting her because it was something a husband was expected to do when his wife was ill. She felt he was only there with her because she was having difficulty in learning to walk and was suffering from loss of memory. Once she could walk, once she could remember perfectly, once she was independent of support he would leave her again. And so she made no effort to improve her walking, made no attempt to remember.

Arrangements were made for her to leave hospital. Her mother brought clothes for her to wear the day before.

'Alun will come for you and you'll go straight to Heathrow,' she said, 'to fly to New York.'

'New York?' exclaimed Jessica. The name of the city jolted her. For some reason she didn't like it. The mists in her mind lifted a little. She saw herself with Alun in a room and she was shouting at him: *You're always going to New York. You're going to see her, aren't you?—that woman. You're having an affair with her!* 'Why are we going to New York? It doesn't appeal to me as a place to have a holiday. Alun said we'd go somewhere quiet, where we would be alone together.'

'Well, you are. From New York you'll catch a plane to an island in the Caribbean. Alun has been lent a villa there by a friend of his. Sounds wonderful, on a cliffside, overlooking a beautiful beach. Quite secluded, he said. And it has a swimming pool so you'll be able to swim and strengthen your spine and legs.'

'Oh.' Jessica felt relief surge through her. 'That sounds better. But clothes—what will I do about clothes? I don't have many suitable for the tropics.'

'I've packed all your summer dresses and your swimsuits. Alun says you'll be able to buy out there. You're going to the French side of St Martin, and he says there are French shops in Marigot, the capital of the French side of the island, where you can buy anything you want. It sounds delightful—a little bit of France set down in the Caribbean Sea. Now I've brought your green tweed to wear tomorrow for flying to New York and you can change when you get there into the thinner clothes I've packed in an overnight bag so that you won't arrive overdressed for the climate in St Martin.'

'But ... but how will I get on to the plane?' quavered Jessica, panicking. 'I ... can't walk very far.'

'Don't worry about it—everything will be taken care of. You'll get preferential treatment. You'll go in a wheelchair on to the plane and be lifted out of it or helped to walk to your seat. Alun has it all arranged—you can depend on him. I'll come in the morning to help you to dress and then go with you both to the airport. Goodnight, dear.' Anthea bent and kissed her. 'Sleep well.'

Jessica didn't sleep well; she was too excited. Her nerves throbbed and her head ached as her imagination ran riot, anticipating the flight to New York, the flight to St Martin, the arrival at a luxurious villa on a cliffside above a beautiful beach. She had never been to the tropics before, of that she was certain. She had never been further south than the Isle of Wight. She slept at last, her dreams filled with waving palm trees and tumbling white surf.

'It will be very different from Wales,' she said to Alun, the next day when they sat in comfortable armchairs on the plane that was taking them across the Atlantic, a silvery dart in the sky demolishing time and space.

'What will?' he asked, and although he spoke casually she felt the sudden tension in him in reaction to her mention of Wales.

'The island of St Martin where we're going,' she replied, gazing out of the window beside her at the bank of clouds far below them, at the brilliant blue of the atmosphere around and above them.

'You remember Wales, then,' he said quietly.

'A little—not much. I remember the mist. White walls shining through grey mist and a plant growing in a garden—love-in-a-mist, I think it's called. There is a garden, isn't there, at the farm?'

'A small one,' he replied cautiously.

'It needed weeding. You don't take care of it properly,' she rebuked him. 'Too busy writing, I suppose.' She looked at him and smiled affection-ately. 'Dai Jones told me it would be better if your farm was amalgamated with his. The two could be managed more efficiently then. . . .' She broke off to stare at him with wide eyes. 'Alun,' she whispered, 'did you hear what I said? I remembered something else about Wales. I remember a man called Dai Jones, and lots of sheep and two dogs. Is there such a man? I haven't imagined him, have I?'

'No. Dai Jones is real and you met him when you were in Wales. His farm is next to mine.'

'Oh, thank goodness for that!' Jessica sank back against the chair back in relief and closed her eyes. Remembering made her tired and now her mind was blank again. She slipped into an uneasy doze.

A few hours later she was looking down on the great American city, its grey and white towers glittering in the pale November sunshine. She was surprised how many trees there were scattered among the buildings. Bridges leapt across ribbons of greyish-blue water linking the island of Manhattan to the surrounding mainland and to Long Island. Big freighters moved slowly under the bridges. The whole scene tilted skywards as the plane banked and turned to make its approach to the land, and then it was gliding swiftly earthwards to merge with its own shadow on the runway.

An hour and a half later they were in another plane and taking off again into the misty blue afternoon light. For a while through the window she could see land, green and yellow fields, thick woodland and glittering rivers, then the cloud enclosed the plane and everything vanished from view.

Jessica sat tensely, keeping her head averted from Alun. Since she had remembered Dai Jones, since she had slept on the other plane, she had remembered much more about Wales. She had remembered why she had gone there. She had gone to ask him for a divorce so that she could marry another man. She couldn't remember yet who that man was, nor could she remember how Alun had answered her request.

She wanted to tell him what she had remembered, but she daren't. If he knew she was remembering Wales and all that had happened there he might think he didn't have to stay with her. He might change his mind about having a holiday with her in a tropical paradise.

So she stayed silent, keeping to herself all that she had remembered about her visit to Wales because she didn't want to know how he had answered her request for a divorce. She didn't want to be divorced from him. She wanted to live with him for the rest of her life because she knew now that she loved him and had always loved him and for as long as she lived there would never be any other man for her. He was her first and only love.

CHAPTER SIX

THE sky was an arch of brilliant blue and above the distant horizon tiny cumulus clouds, like newly risen mushrooms, rolled lazily. The air was warm but not humid, scented with the perfumes of exotic plants and the faint salty tang of the sea. On a beach far below and unseen, surf whispered lazily to the hot sun-kissed sand.

Lying on a lounger on a stone terrace that seemed to hang between sky and sea, halfway down a craggy cliff, Jessica was sunbathing, her fair lightly tanned skin smothered in lotion, her head covered by a woven straw hat. She was lying on her stomach and was trying to read a book that she had propped up against a cushion.

But the book wasn't holding her attention. The antics of the espionage agents in the highly-touted best-seller were too violent, too far-fetched to interest her, and with a sigh born of boredom she flicked the book closed and turning on to her back, sat up to face the sea. It was bright blue, flecked with the crests of waves, and although she was wearing sunglasses she had to shade her eyes with one hand against the dazzle of the westering sun on the water. Against the dazzle she could just make out the shape of a small sail, a dark triangle above the gleaming shape of a sailboard.

While she watched the sail grew bigger as it

came closer to the land and she was able to make out its colours, orange with a double yellow stripe. She could also see the dark figure of the person who was sailing the windsurfer as he bent his knees and pulled on the boom of the sail, balancing the board at the same time as bringing the sail as close to the wind as possible. She knew he was Alun, enjoying one of the outdoor activities at which he excelled.

The small sail craft passed from her view, hidden by the spur of rock jutting out a few feet below the terrace where a kidney-shaped swimming pool glittered, like a turquoise jewel caught between rough crags of yellow sandstone. She leaned back and closed her eyes with a sigh. Soon Alun would come to the terrace to find her, to ask her how she was feeling. He would probe gently and with consideration, and after she had answered him he would sit for a while with her and the tension would build up between them, slowly and inevitably, until one of them decided to move, finding an excuse to leave the other and go into the house or down to the beach.

With a little exclamation of distress Jessica sat up again and stared out at the blue, sun-glinting Caribbean Sea. She and Alun had been at King's Fancy, as the villa was so fancifully called, for nearly two weeks now. Another week to go and then they would have to return to England. The holiday that had been planned to restore her to complete health would be over. She would go back to work for Lithgow's Ltd as a furniture designer and Alun would . . . go where? Back to Wales?

Back to Whitewalls to start an adventure school with Mavis Owen? She didn't know because he hadn't mentioned his plans to her. She didn't know because she hadn't asked him what he was going to do. She hadn't asked because she hadn't told him that she could remember everything that had happened in Wales and during the two years of their separation. She was afraid to tell him because she guessed that once he knew her memory had returned, he would leave her. While he believed she was still incapacitated he would stay with her, playing the part of the considerate and attentive husband.

She groaned and hid her face in her hands. This stay in a tropical paradise, this holiday from which she had hoped to gain so much, had turned out to be a sort of hell for her. And all of her own creation, because she couldn't bring herself to tell Alun the truth.

Two weeks of being together and yet not being together, because he had given her the kid-glove treatment, never once showing a desire to make love to her. The kisses they had exchanged had been brief tokens of affection exchanged at meetings and partings, in the morning at the breakfast table, at night when they went to their separate bedrooms.

At first she had understood why he hadn't shared her bedroom. She had still been recovering her strength and she had appreciated his restraint. But now it seemed to her that he didn't want to make love to her. Why? The answer came to her clearly. Because he didn't love her any more. He didn't want her to be his wife any more, and once this was over, once he was sure she was fully recovered, he would start talking about a divorce.

He was kind, kinder than she had ever believed he could be, but there were times when she found his kindness cruel and she longed for him to behave normally, to torment her with words, to laugh at her, but most of all she wanted him to make love to her again. She ached for his touch, for the feel of him inside her. Oh, she was healthy again, with every part of her body functioning as it should and every emotion clamouring to be expressed.

He came, stepping out from the house behind the terrace. Barefooted, and wearing only brief white shorts, his compact torso tanned to a teak colour, he was carrying two tall glasses in which ice-cubes clinked. Both were filled to the brim almost with yellow-orange fruit juice spiked with rum. He handed one of the glasses to Jessica and dragging one of the deck chairs closer to her lounger with one foot he sat down in it. He raised his glass to her and then took a long sip of the drink.

'So what have you been doing this afternoon?' he asked.

'Reading.'

'No swimming?'

'No.'

'You should do it every day.'

'I'm tired of swimming, especially by myself,' Jessica retorted.

'You could have come windsurfing with me.'

'I don't know how to sail.'

'You could learn.'

There was a short tense silence. They were on the verge of quarrelling. She could sense Alun's irritation with her. In other circumstances, if he had been behaving normally it would have boiled over by now and he would have treated her to a show of his wild Welsh temper. Inaction was something he couldn't understand and never had. Always he had to be doing something; climbing, riding, swimming, sailing, writing, exploring. The past two weeks staying with her, helping her to recuperate, must have been hell for him too.

'Alun?'

'Mmm?' He was sipping through the straw in his glass and didn't look up at her, seemingly more interested in watching the liquid in the glass go down as he sipped. The thick black fringes of his lashes concealed his eyes. His golden-brown skin gleamed in the sunlight. His shapely sinewy legs were stretched before him. Jessica felt a sharp stab of desire somewhere in the lower regions of her body. She swallowed hard and her hands clenched on her knees.

'Supposing ... supposing,' she muttered, 'my memory doesn't come back completely. Supposing I never remember what happened since ... since you returned from South America, what ... What will you do?'

Alun took his time about answering. He finished his drink, slowly drawing the liquid up through the straw, savouring it and all the time watching the level go lower in the glass, then blowing bubbles in it rather boyishly when there was only a little left. Jessica found she was clenching her hands even more tightly. His behaviour was subtly annoying. She longed to reach across, snatch the glass from him and force him to look at her, insist that he answer her question. At last he sat up, put the empty glass on the small glass-topped table that was between them and with his elbows in his knees, hands cupping his chin, he looked at her, his golden eyes clear and wide open as they searched her face.

'Are you sure you haven't remembered anything else about that period of time?' he queried coolly. 'Seems to me you were remembering quite a lot about Wales when we were on the plane flying here. Haven't you had any more flashbacks?'

Confronted by such direct questions, she withdrew hastily, leaning back, looking down at her own drink, only half-consumed.

'Wouldn't I have told you if I had?' she countered shakily.

'I don't know. Would you?' he replied dryly, and she flashed an uneasy glance in his direction.

'You haven't answered my question,' she retorted. 'Would you mind if I never remember the past two years?'

'Don't you mean would I mind if you decided you'd preferred not to remember?' he asked, his voice even drier. 'I'm not sure. I'll have to think about it,' he added, getting to his feet. 'Like another drink?'

'No, thanks.'

'I would,' he said, and left her, striding up the

wide shallow steps and disappearing in behind the oleander bushes that screened the entrance to the lounge, a long wide room without walls or windows, open on two sides to the trade winds that provided natural air-conditioning; a beautiful room furnished with simple bamboo and teak furniture, its floor covered with cool tiles.

Alone on the terrace again, Jessica sipped her drink and waited for him to return. She was no nearer to knowing what he would do if she confessed that she remembered what had happened in the past two years; if she told him she knew they had been discussing divorce when they had been in Wales.

By the time she had finished her drink Alun hadn't come back to the terrace, so she went into the house too. He wasn't in the living room, so she went through the room and along a passage that had windows without glass, open to the air, that could be closed with wooden shutters whenever the weather deteriorated, something that only happened in the summer when the rains came and the hurricanes, she had been told.

The passage led to the suite of rooms that she and Alun had used since they had arrived, two bedrooms and a bathroom and a small sitting room. None of the rooms had glass windows, only shutters. There were no doors either. Colours were cool, imitating the shades of the sea, palest aquamarine right through to deepest purple. The two bedrooms were separated by the bathroom.

Passing the entrance to her own bedroom, Jessica walked past the bathroom with its sliding

screen door and straight to Alun's room. He
wasn't there. Only the pair of white shorts he had
been wearing lay on the floor where he had tossed
them, evidence that he had been there, had
changed his clothes and had gone . . . where?

Biting her lip, inwardly chiding herself for being
upset because he hadn't returned to the terrace to
talk to her or just be with her, because he had
gone out somewhere without her and hadn't told
her where he would be going, Jessica drifted back
to her own bedroom and flopped down on the
smooth bed that was covered with cool flowered
Sea Island cotton. Overhead the fan attached to
the ceiling whirred quietly.

Her spirits plummeting to the lowest point since
she had been in hospital in England, she lay there for
a long time, too unhappy to move. She was trapped
in a situation of her own making. She had been
deceiving Alun for nearly two weeks, and he had
guessed that she had. Originally her amnesia had
been caused, as Dr Mehta had suggested, by a
refusal to face up to something that had caused her
distress and pain. That something had been her
separation from Alun and the knowledge that he
would have let her have a divorce so he could go into
business with Mavis Owen. That knowledge still
gave her acute distress and pain and she was still
refusing to face up to its reality by pretending she
didn't remember, hoping that Alun would forget too.

But instead of their relationship returning to the
way it had been before they had been separated, it
had deteriorated. They weren't any closer to each
other. They were like strangers, polite strangers,

living under the same roof, living a lie—a lie that was driving them further and further apart.

The room grew darker as the sun set. Outside among the shrubs frogs began their repetitive refrain. The tropical night, mysteriously exciting, had begun. She rose from the bed and went to the bathroom. She showered and then returned to her room to dress in a plain dress made from red cotton. It was almost seven o'clock, the time when the evening meal was always served. Surely Alun would come back for that?

But he wasn't in the lounge, nor was he on the terrace beyond, and he hadn't come by the time the maid came to tell Jessica that dinner was ready to be served if she would like to go through to the dining room.

Like the lounge, the dining room was open on two sides so that air could waft through. Candles in glass bowls glimmered, the flames occasionally flaring when the breeze whispered through. White lace mats made delicate web-like patterns on the dark polished surface of the table and heavy silverware gleamed in the candlelight. There were two places set.

'Mr Gower, he phone from the airport,' said the maid. 'He say to tell you not to wait dinner for him. He say the plane he gone to meet late. He be here in half an hour.'

'Oh, good. Thank you,' said Jessica, feeling relief. Alun hadn't gone for good, then. She wondered whom he had gone to meet off a plane.

'You want me to bring food in now?' asked the maid.

'Yes, please.' She realised suddenly that she was very hungry and wondered how much her low spirits had been due to hunger.

She would tell Alun tonight, she decided, as she forked up the delicious prawn cocktail. She would tell him that she remembered everything . . . or at least nearly everything that had happened during the past two years. She would say it simply, not telling him exact incidents or conversations. She would just say, 'I remember,' and wait for him to react. Yes, that would be the best way. She couldn't go on the way they were. She had to open the doors of communication between them somehow; the situation would only become more tense if she didn't.

Her appetite spiced by her decision, she ate everything that was put before her—the prawn cocktail, the salad, the grilled grouper fish served with tiny potatoes and broccoli, the strawberries Romanoff, and she drank two glasses of white wine. She felt suddenly lighthearted, as if she were celebrating an occasion. The occasion of the return of her memory. She smiled a little wryly at the thought and then was overwhelmed by a sudden longing for Alun, wishing he were there to celebrate with her.

She had finished eating and was sitting in the lounge pretending to read when she heard voices, a woman's, low and deep, first and then Alun's even deeper answering. The sound came from the terrace and Jessica looked up, feeling her heart leap as it always did when she knew Alun was near.

They came up the wide shallow steps together, the tall woman who was wearing a finely woven straw hat over a bandeau that swathed her head, concealing her hair, and Alun, slightly taller than the woman, his deep tan set off by the white shirt and pants he was wearing, the silvery streak in his dark hair catching the light. They were laughing and they seemed to be very friendly, Jessica thought, and felt jealousy uncoil within her.

The woman, who was very thin, was also very elegant, wearing close-fitting white pants that emphasised the graceful line of her long legs and a shocking pink loose shirt with long full sleeves. Gold chains glinted within the open neck of the shirt and gold bracelets jangled on one of her thin wrists. As she reached the top step she looked across the room and saw Jessica and came straight towards her, walking with a strangely pantherish gliding stride that was vaguely familiar. Jessica got politely to her feet and smiled uncertainly. A long thin hand was stretched out towards her. A thin lined face smiled at her. Tawny eyes glinted between dark lashes. The woman was much older than she had thought, over fifty, possibly near sixty.

'You must be Jessica,' the woman said. 'I'm so pleased to meet you at last. I'm Ashley King.'

The last mists that lingered in Jessica's mind swirled violently and were gone, dispersed by a blinding light.

'How do you do,' she murmured, feeling her hand being squeezed by thin fingers. 'You ... you're from New York. Alun often goes to see you.' She caught her breath in a gasp as she realised what she had just said. She had remembered something new, something that had been well hidden in the depths of her subconscious. She had remembered that she and Alun had quarrelled about this woman. One hand to her mouth, she glanced straight at Alun, who was standing behind Ashley King. He was looking right at her, his eyes gleaming with mockery.

Pulling her hand sharply away from Ashley's, she turned and ran down the steps of the terrace, then swerving left hurried down more steps to a wide driveway where two cars were parked in front of garage doors. Out between gateposts built of brown stone she ran into a lane, then turning to the right she went down the lane to the beach.

The soft sand sank under her feet as she walked beside the glittering surf, trying to deal with the shock she had felt on being introduced to Ashley King. How could Alun have done this to her? How could he have been so cruel as to confront her with the woman whose lover he had been? And now he knew that she was no longer suffering from loss of memory. She had given herself away with her recognition of Ashley King's name and by her remark that Ashley was from New York. He had tricked her into betraying herself. The least he could have done would have been to warn her that afternoon that Ashley was coming to visit him.

Was Ashley going to stay at the villa? Oh God, she hoped not. She didn't think she could put up with a *ménage à trois*; herself, Alun, and his elderly lover. Sickness surged up in her as her puritan instincts were revolted by even the suggestion of perversion. She would have to leave. She would leave now, pack her bags and get Pierre to drive her into Marigot to stay at a hotel there. Better still, drive into Philipsburg and stay there. It was the bigger town, more cosmopolitan, and it would be easier to hide in, and tomorrow she would make arrangements to fly back to England somehow. She had money of her own, thank God—her mother had seen to that.

The decision made, she made her way back to the house, approaching the suite of rooms by a path that twisted through the shrubbery so that she wouldn't have to meet Ashley King or Alun again. In her bedroom she quickly began to pack her clothing. She had packed one case and was rapidly filling the other when Alun strolled into the room. He leaned against the wall just inside the doorway, folding his arms across his chest.

'You were very rude just now, leaving us without a word,' he said coldly. 'Where did you go?'

'I felt sick. I went for a walk on the beach. To clear my head,' Jessica replied stiffly, continuing with her packing.

'And what are you doing now?'

'Can't you see?' She was deliberately acid. 'I'm packing. I can't stay here any longer. I can't stay while that . . . that woman from New York is in the house.' Her voice shook a little and her hands were still. Distress that he could insult her by inviting Ashley King to come and stay in the same house as herself welled up inside her; that he, whom she loved so much, could be so depraved.

'That woman, as you call her, happens to be the owner of this house,' he drawled quietly. 'And I didn't invite her. She always comes to stay here at this time of the year.'

'Oh.' Her hands began to move again, folding and re-folding a peach-coloured underslip. She hardly knew what she was doing, she was so upset. 'It doesn't make any difference. I'm still leaving,' she muttered.

'Because your memory has come back?' he asked jeeringly. 'Because you've remembered we'd been living apart for two years before you came to see me in Wales? Because you've remembered you want to divorce me so you can marry someone else? Is that why you're leaving?' His voice had taken on the soft menacing sibilance which warned that his temper was fast reaching boiling point, and Jessica glanced up warily. Alun was moving towards her and his eyes were blazing with anger and something else; something that seemed very close to hatred. 'You've been lying to me, haven't you? All the time you've been here you've been lying, pretending you couldn't remember; playing on my sympathy and at the same time keeping me at arm's length. . . .'

'I . . . was going to tell you the truth tonight,' she whispered, backing away from him. 'Honestly I was, Alun. I . . . I've remembered everything . . . but I . . . I hadn't remembered Ashley. I'd forgotten about her, and when I saw her it was as if a blinding light blazed through my mind and I

... I remembered you'd been having an affair with her and that was why we quarrelled, why you stayed away from me all this time. Oh, how could you, Alun? How could you have an affair with her? She's old enough to be your mother!'

'She *is* my mother, you stupid little bitch!' he hissed at her, and grabbing hold of her he dragged her against his hard lean body, and holding her face with cruelly biting fingers he bent his head and blistered her lips with the heat and hardness of his own.

There was nothing loving or tender in the way he kissed her. His intent was to punish her, and he did, pressing his mouth against hers until her own sharp teeth cut into the soft flesh, drawing blood. Around her body his hard lean arms tightened so much that she was afraid he would crack one of her ribs and he thrust a leg roughly between her knees, forcing them apart. Hate was his motive for doing what he was doing to her, not love, and she struggled with all the strength she had to free herself without success.

Across the flat cotton-cool surface of the bed they fell, and Jessica managed to free her mouth from the domination of his to gasp.

'Alun, no! Please wait. Let me explain. I didn't know you ... you never told me about your mother. ...'

'No explanations. No more excuses,' he panted, his eyes flaming with golden fire. 'You're mine, and by God, I'm going to have you here and now! You can't keep me at arm's length any more with your lies!'

He'd gone mad. She had driven him to madness, was the overriding thought running through her mind as his lips claimed hers again. And what was the best way to deal with a madman? It was to humour him, wasn't it? Go part way along the path he wanted to tread.

But he made her go with him all the way, and she couldn't resist his kisses or the caresses of his long fingers on her arms, her legs, her body. Her mind reeling with sensuousness, she was more than ready for him when he took her, and culmination for her was just as much a shuddering explosion of passion as it was for him, leaving her limp and moaning, bruised and shaken, incapable of coherent speech, completely vanquished.

Dawn was breaking, pale light slanting into the room, when Jessica moved at last, coming to the surface of a deep sleep, disturbed by some noise. Above the fan whirred softly. For a few moments she lay aware that she was alone, that someone had laid her against pillows and had covered her with a sheet, and slowly the memory of what had happened in the night trickled into her mind.

Well, she had got what she had been longing for, hadn't she? She had wanted Alun and she had got him—in fury and frustration, it was true. Sighing, she licked her lips. They were bruised and throbbing. She supposed she should feel ashamed and angry at the way it had happened, because he had taken her in anger and not in love. But she didn't, because she had felt the same as he had, fury and frustration at the situation in which they had both been trapped.

She wished he had stayed with her, though, then they could have talked. She could have made those explanations she had wanted to make and he had refused to let her make, closing her mouth with his hot demanding kisses. And she could have asked him about his mother, Ashley King. She could have asked him why Sally had never told her that Ashley King was his mother.

Perhaps they could talk now. Jessica turned and looked at the unshuttered window opening. The sky was growing lighter, streaked with pink. She pushed the sheet from her and swung off the bed. From the case where she had packed it the previous night she took her blue and white cotton dressing gown and wrapped it around her nakedness. Shaking her hair back from her face, she padded past the bathroom and into Alun's room.

In the greyness of dawn the room looked bleak, devoid of colour. The double bed was smooth, untouched. He wasn't there and it looked very much as if he hadn't been there. She felt a flicker of panic. Where was he? Surely he hadn't left. Suddenly she was running to the closet, sliding back the doors. A few clothes were hanging there. But hadn't he brought more with him? And where was his lightweight flight bag, the one he always took with him when he had to fly somewhere on an assignment?

Although she searched the room thoroughly she couldn't find that bag. Nor could she find some of his clothing; the heavy working denims, the tough denim shirts, the jungle boots.

Puzzled, she went into the bathroom. Sunrise flooded the room with peach-coloured light. Steam still shrouded the mirror and water still dripped from the shower tap. It wasn't long since someone had been in there. Maybe Alun hadn't left yet. Maybe he was having breakfast, planning on returning to her room to wake her up and say goodbye to her, tell her where he was going.

She hurried along the passage. He wasn't in the lounge, he wasn't in the breakfast room and there was no one in the kitchen cooking. Jessica went back to the lounge and stepped out on to the terrace. Sea and sky were flushed flamingo pink now and in the distance the horizon was a smudged violet line. Birds were singing among the exotic, sweet-smelling shrubs and some were flitting about, swooping through the open lounge. Alun wasn't there.

She was just thinking of returning to her room when she heard the sound of a car's engine as the vehicle turned into the driveway. She went down the steps to the driveway. The dark blue Cadillac was just stopping. The engine was turned off, a door opened and Pierre got out, big and burly, his shiny brown head fringed with greying curls. He came towards the steps whistling cheerfully. When he saw Jessica he stopped abruptly, his big eyes opening wide. A white-toothed smile slashed his brown face.

'Good morning, missus,' he drawled. 'You're up early this morning. You feeling much better now?'

'Good morning. Yes, I am feeling better, much better, thank you. Where have you been?'

'I just took Mr Gower to the airport to catch the early morning flight to Miami.' He cocked his head to one side and glanced skywards. 'I guess that's his plane taking off right now. Can you hear the roar of the engine.'

She could hear the distinctive noise of a jetliner taking off and she also looked skywards. In a few seconds the silvery plane appeared flying past, its nose in the air as it ascended. Aware that Pierre has gone into the house, Jessica stood where she was watching the plane until it was out of sight. Then slowly and thoughtfully she returned to her bedroom.

There was no note on the dressing table. Alun had gone without a word, without a parting kiss. Having found out that her memory had returned, knowing that she was back to full strength and well able to take care of herself, he had gone, probably on an assignment for the magazine for which his mother worked as an editor.

His mother. Ashley King was his mother and was owner of this house, King's Fancy. But why had she never known? Why had no one told her? Why had Sally let her think that Ashley King was younger and Alun's mistress? Why hadn't Alun himself told her about his mother?

Oh, she knew that answer to that last question, she thought as she made her way back to her room. Nosy questions about his family had been taboo in their relationship. That had been part of their arrangement. They had married each other, not a family, not each other's parents, sisters or brothers, Alun had once said to her. Family had

been something he hadn't wanted to know about
and had apparently not wanted to tell her about.

She showered and dressed in shorts and
sleeveless shirt and hung up the clothes she had
packed the previous night. There was no need to
run away quite so precipitately now. She could
make arrangements for her departure to England
in a more leisurely fashion once she knew where
Alun had gone.

'Good morning, Jessica.' Ashley King, dressed
as simply yet as elegantly as she had been the
previous evening in well-fitting lilac-coloured
pants, a flowered-patterned long-sleeved shirt
made from cotton and a lilac scarf swathed around
her head, its ends tied at the back, was sitting at a
table on the terrace where Pierre was serving her
breakfast. 'And how are you feeling today?'
Ashley smiled, showing that she still had very
good teeth.

'Good morning,' murmured Jessica, feeling
suddenly shy and uncomfortable now that she
knew who Ashley was. She slid on to the chair that
Pierre pulled back for her. 'I'm feeling very well,
thank you, Mrs King. . . .'

'Please call me Ashley. I'm not *Mrs* King nor
Mrs anything else. King is my family name, just as
Martin is yours.'

'Ashley, then. I . . . I just wanted to say I'm
sorry I was rude yesterday evening. It was a
shock meeting you so suddenly. You see, I'd
forgotten. . . .' Jessica broke off pink with embar-
rassment as she remembered what it was she had
forgotten—or rather, what she had deliberately

closed her mind to. She had once believed that
Alun had had an affair with a woman called
Ashley King and she had quarrelled with him
about it.

'Alun explained to me,' said Ashley, smiling
again. 'About your loss of memory after the
accident.' The smile faded and Ashley looked
suitably sympathetic. 'It must have been a terrible
time for you. But I'm glad you're better now. I
know Alun has been very concerned about you
and quite disappointed that your stay here didn't
seem to be helping your memory much. He knew,
you see, that he couldn't stay with you until the
end of the month, but he didn't want to leave
you on your own. That's why he phoned me and
asked me if I'd come and stay with you for a while
so he could go off to New Guinea to join
Bruce Kerowski there. Bruce is one of our best
photographers and together they've been compiling
information about rain forests which the magazine
is featuring in next March's edition.'

'Oh, I see,' said Jessica stiffly. Pierre had
brought her fruit juice and her own separate pot of
coffee. She ordered croissants and strawberry
preserve and he went away. She sipped some
orange juice and then said quickly before she
could change her mind, 'I didn't know until last
night that you're Alun's mother.'

'You didn't?' Ashley's glance expressed surprise.
Then she laughed. 'How like Alun not to tell you!
He's really very secretive, as you must have found
out over the years. That's the Welsh in him. Huw
was like that too—fiercely proud and independent

and never letting anyone know his thoughts and feelings ... except in poetry.' Ashley paused and then added, 'That lovely lyrical poetry of his that none of us could understand except in translation because it was all written in Welsh.' She looked across at Jessica. 'You did meet him, didn't you?'

'Yes, once. Not for long.' Pierre came with the croissants and jam. She poured herself some coffee and slit open a croissant, wondering how she could ask her next question without seeming to be too curious. 'I stayed in his house too, last June. Alun was living there.'

'Whitewalls?' asked Ashley, her eyes dreamy. 'I stayed there too, before and after Alun was born. It's a pretty place, but I couldn't have lived there. It was too remote for me, too misty and mysterious.' Her faint smile mocked herself. 'I'm strictly a city bird, and that city has to be the Big Apple. I can only stay here for a short time.'

'Is ... is that why you left him—Huw Gower, I mean?' ventured Jessica tentatively. 'Because you couldn't live where he wanted to live?'

Across the table Ashley studied Jessica's face with narrowed eyes.

'Alun hasn't told you anything, has he?' she remarked. 'He's just expected you to understand him without you knowing anything.' She sighed and leaned back in her chair.

'Then I guess I'd better fill you in on a few things.' She smiled again, an ironic quirk of the lips that was familiar to Jessica. Alun had inherited it. 'After all, that's what a mother-in-law is for, isn't it?' Ashley laughed outright this time.

'You know, being a mother-in-law is the last role I would ever have cast for myself. I was very surprised when Alun told me he'd got married. Marriage didn't seem to be his life-style at all.'

'That's what other people have said about him,' said Jessica.

'What other people?'

'His sister Margian and Sally Fairbourne, his cousin.'

'Hmm. Well, Margian would know him as well as anyone, I guess. After all, he grew up with her at Whitewalls. But this cousin Sally, who is she? I don't seem to have heard of her.'

'I'm not sure of the actual relationship, but her family used to live near my home in Beechfield. It was at the Fairbourne house that I met Alun.'

'I don't know them at all. You see, I was never married to Huw,' said Ashley coolly.

'Not married?' gasped Jessica.

'He was married to someone else, to Margian's mother, and she might have been a Fairbourne for all I know. She died, unfortunately, soon after Margian was born. I met Huw when I was attending an English university, taking a post-graduate course. He came to give a talk on the influence of Welsh rhythms and imagery on poets who had written in English.' Ashley's eyes grew dreamy again as she looked into the past. 'Even now I can remember the impact he had. He was about forty at the time, tall and black-haired, with a handsome haggard face—he was still mourning the death of his wife. He looked, I suppose, like the romantic poet he was. I fell in love with him and made every effort to get to know him. To my surprise he responded and invited me to visit him in Wales. I went to Whitewalls and stayed for a while. We were very happy together.'

'Then why didn't you stay with him for ever?'

'He didn't ask me to,' replied Ashley. 'He was, I guess, still in love with his first wife. As for me, I'm very independent, too, and I had my life all planned. I wanted to return to New York to work for the magazine my father had helped to found. I wasn't interested in domesticity.' Her lips curved in an ironic smile. 'I was extremely annoyed when I realised I was pregnant. I could have concealed the fact and had an abortion, I guess, but that thought didn't enter my head. The child I had conceived was the result of my love for Huw, so when Alun was born I wrote to Huw and told him. He was delighted to have a son and said I was to take Alun to him, to live with him and to grow up in Wales. And that is what happened. I took Alun to Huw. Margian was three at the time, and I don't think she has ever known Alun is not her full brother. Only one other person over there knows that I'm Alun's mother, Huw's close friend and neighbour, David Jones. And now you know. Does knowing make a difference to you, Jessica?'

'Yes, it does. You see, Sally Fairbourne once told me that Alun was having an affair with a woman called Ashley King. I believed her and was very upset. Alun and I quarrelled about it and he left. We'd been separated for nearly two years when I was hurt in that accident.'

'So he has told me. He told me too that you

went to see him in Wales to ask for a divorce. Do you still want one?'

'If he wants one I'll agree,' Jessica muttered. 'I don't want to come between him and what he wants to do. I love him too much to do that.'

'But I had the impression it's you who really wants the divorce, so you can marry someone else; someone who would be a better husband, stay with you all the time, give you security and children. Is that what you want?' asked Ashley, looking puzzled.

Jessica frowned and bit her lip as she played with the remains of a croissant on her plate. After a while she looked up and straight at Ashley.

She's a beautiful woman, she thought, *and she must have been even more beautiful thirty-seven years ago when she first met Huw Gower. She's strong too— stronger than I am or will ever be. Strong enough to make a life for herself without the man she loved. Strong enough to give up her own child. I don't think I could do that. I'm too possessive, I realise that now. I want Alun to be a part of my life always and I want to be the mother of his children and mine. I suppose I'm just plain old-fashioned.*

'Say what you feel, Jessica,' Ashley prompted softly. 'Don't hide from the truth about yourself.'

'I . . . I'd like to have Alun in my life always,' Jessica confessed diffidently, 'but I'm afraid that if . . . if I show I'm possessive about him, he'll leave again and won't come back to me. I love him very much and I would like to have his children. I don't want to be married to anyone else, and I have no need to be now.'

'Then you must tell Alun when he returns from New Guinea, because I don't think he knows how you feel,' advised Ashley gently.

'But ... he might not come back to me when he's finished his assignment,' muttered Jessica. 'I can't be sure he'll come to me now. You see, he wasn't very pleased with me last night and he left this morning without telling me where he was going, without saying goodbye.'

'I know he did. And I was very annoyed with him for leaving without speaking to you. He came to see me before he rushed off to the airport. He said you were so fast asleep he didn't have the heart to disturb you. He'd overslept and was afraid he'd miss the plane. He asked me to explain to you and to tell you he'll contact you as soon as he can. He'll be returning as soon as he and Bruce have enough information and pictures to finish the series of articles. That won't be until after Christmas.' Ashley paused, then added, 'You could stay here until he comes if you like. You're very welcome to stay.'

'Oh no. It's lovely here, I like the house, the island and the people, but I must go back to Beechfield now that I'm well enough. I want to go back to do my own work. I have a job, too, as a furniture designer,' Jessica replied.

'Yes, I know, and I fully appreciate your desire to return to work. But you'll stay another week, please. It will give us time to get to know each other better, and I think it's time I got to know you, Jessica.'

'Thank you, I'd like to stay with you,' replied Jessica sincerely.

CHAPTER SEVEN

A WEEK later Jessica left St Martin, seen off at Juliana airport by Ashley. In the early morning of the next day she arrived at Heathrow and was met by her mother.

'You're looking so much better!' exclaimed Anthea. 'But you must put a coat on before we go out to the car. It's freezing outside—an unexpected cold spell.'

Trees, fields and hedges were all rimed with frost that sparkled under the rays of a pale yellow sun. Looking out of the car window while her mother drove, Jessica felt as if she had been away for years instead of only three weeks. Then she remembered that before she had gone to the Caribbean she hadn't really been in Buckinghamshire or Beechfield; not so as to know she was, anyway. She had been in limbo, because that was what living without a memory in hospital had been like.

Six whole months had gone by since she had set out for Wales to see Alun, and in that time she had changed. *Then* she had been uncertain and vulnerable, easily influenced by what other people had said about Alun, because she hadn't known about herself. She hadn't known what it was she wanted from life or from him. *Now* she knew, and she was prepared to be patient with him, to wait

for him to come back to her and, when he came, to
tell him how she felt.

She had had a wonderful week staying at King's
Fancy with Ashley. Cool and casual, Ashley had
made an ideal companion, taking her to visit other
New Yorkers who owned luxurious hideaway
villas; one a well-known jazz musician who lived at
a place called Oyster Cove; another a TV producer
and another who was the author of several bestselling books, some of which had been made into
successful films. And everywhere they had visited
Ashley had introduced her merely as a young
friend of hers from England.

'No one has to know about our relationship,'
she had said. 'After all, none of them know that Alun
is my son. It's none of their business. I don't ask if
the younger people who are staying at their villas
are their children or their grandchildren, nor do I
want to know. Personal privacy is something that
is very sacred to me. It was to Huw, too. I hope,
Jessica, you will respect it too and not tell anyone
in England I'm Alun's mother.'

'Not even my mother?' Jessica had asked.

'Not even your mother. Can you do it?'

'Yes, I promise.'

She glanced now sideways at Anthea. She would
never tell her because she knew that Anthea would
be shocked to learn that Alun had been born
illegitimately. And never in a million years would
Anthea understand Ashley. Giving up her child,
letting him grow up half-wild among the Welsh
mountains supervised in his formative years by a
reclusive sheepfarmer-poet, would be beyond

Anthea's comprehension. Conventional to her back-bone, she would disapprove strongly of Ashley's life-style. She probably disapproved of Alun's too, and wished her daughter had never married him.

The house in Beechfield looked just the same as always, its red brick glowing softly in the winter sunshine, the roses in the front garden still blooming in spite of the pinch of frost.

'I expect you'll want to rest today,' said Anthea as she made tea in the kitchen. 'I'll be going to work as usual. Okay?'

'I'll come to the factory with you. It's time I found out just exactly what job Arthur Lithgow wants me to do. Mother, have you seen anything of Chris Pollet lately?'

'Oh, you've remembered him, have you?' said Anthea, looking rather uncomfortable.

'Of course I have. I've remembered everything. I've remembered that he was interested in helping us when we were in such a bind about the bank foreclosing.'

'Was he? You didn't tell me that.'

'I know I didn't. He ... well, he had certain conditions I would have had to meet, and I wasn't sure whether I could.'

'So that was why he was so cool when I met him one day at a furniture manufacturers' association meeting,' remarked Anthea, frowning into her tea-cup.

'When was that? When did you see him?' asked Jessica.

'About two weeks ago. He asked after you and I

told him you were on holiday in the Caribbean. He was surprised and wanted to know when you'd be returning to work. You know, Jessica, I never cared much for your association with him,' her mother went on. 'I've always felt that he isn't as straightforward as he likes to seem. By the way, where's Alun? Why hasn't he come back with you?'

'He's in New Guinea, on an assignment. He'll be home in the New Year.'

'What do you mean by home? Do you mean he'll go back to Wales? Or will he be coming here?'

'He'll be coming here or wherever I am,' said Jessica positively. That was something else she had learned, she thought, to be and to behave positively. Everything was much more likely to work out the way you wanted it to be if you took a positive attitude to life.

'Then should I assume you're together again?' asked Anthea. 'No more living apart except when he's away on assignment, of course.'

'Yes, you can assume that.'

'I'm glad. I like Alun—I felt a soft spot for him when your father used to rant about him having seduced you. I've always felt that in spite of his strange way of living, fundamentally he's a strong person who would come through in a crisis. And he did. He came when he heard you were in a mess and he took over, took you away for a holiday, gave you the support you needed to recover completely. I hope you're going to stay married to him, Jess.'

'I'm going to try,' Jessica whispered. 'It . . . it's

really up to him now whether he wants to stay married to me.'

Returning to work at the furniture factory was much easier than she had anticipated it would be. Although now a subsidiary of Lithgows, Martin and Son Ltd hadn't been changed. The same people were working there who had been working there when her father had died and no one had been taken on in her position in the design department. Within a few days she was settled in and feeling as if she had never been away.

The days grew shorter and darker. Christmas came and went with the usual office parties, neighbourhood parties, gift-giving, and Christmas Day spent quietly at home with Anthea. Jessica received a card from Ashley with a note in it saying that Alun's assignment was successful and on schedule. She heard nothing from him, and as the time went by, the year changing, the days lengthening, January giving way to February, with no word of his return the old doubts and fears began to clamour in her mind.

Suppose he didn't come back to her? Suppose he had returned already and had gone straight to Wales, to Mavis Owen and her plans for starting an adventure school? Suppose he hadn't forgiven her for pretending her memory hadn't returned while they had stayed together in St Martin? Suppose he didn't want to be married to her any longer? Suppose, suppose . . . she was nearly out of her mind with suppositions and had to make a determined effort to close her mind to them.

At the beginning of February she moved out of

her mother's house and into a pleasant flat in one of Beechfield's few high-rise buildings. She moved as much to get away from her mother's influence as to give herself something to do furnishing the flat, pretending to herself that she had to make a home for Alun to come back to. She had been in the flat a week when she ran into Chris Pollet at a nearby shopping centre.

'It's good to see you again, Jess,' he said warmly, shaking her hand. 'I can see you're fully recovered now. That was quite a scare you gave your mother.'

'Oh, you know about the accident?'

'Of course. I sent you flowers, but I guess you didn't notice them. You were in a coma for a while, weren't you?'

'Yes, but. . . .' She frowned in puzzlement. 'Why didn't you come to visit me when I was getting better; when I was out of the coma?'

'Well now, that's a long story,' he replied with a wry curve to his mouth. 'For one thing, your mother was very protective of you, wouldn't let me come near you.' He glanced around at the shopping precinct. 'Look, we can't talk here. How about dinner tonight?'

'I'd like that. Where?'

'There's a nice little place out at Winkleford, The Waggoner's Arms, really old. Parts of it Elizabethan, they say. They just have a few tables and the food is superb. Are you still living in Wordsworth Close? Shall I pick you up from there, say, about seven?'

'No, I'm living here, in the town,' Jessica told him. 'Six-fourteen Beechfield Towers.'

'On your own?' His grey glance was sharp and wary.

'At the moment, yes,' she replied coolly. 'I'll be waiting for you in the entrance hall to the building at seven. See you later.'

As always when she returned to the flat she opened her mailbox on the ground floor hopefully; hoping to find a letter or a card from Alun. But there were only bills.

Oh, why did she bother? she wondered as she let herself into the flat. He didn't care for her. If he did he would do everything he could to keep in touch with her somehow, either through the magazine's headquarters in New York, or through his mother.

Maybe she was wasting her time being faithful to him, waiting for him, hoping that their problem was resolved and that they were going to live happily ever after. Maybe she would be better off divorcing him and marrying someone else; someone like Chris Pollet. Maybe she just wasn't suited to the sort of marriage Alun wanted, an open affair in which they were both free to come and go as they pleased; free to go out with or even have an affair with someone else. Maybe she should never have married him in the first place.

What was marriage but commitment legalised? she argued with herself as she changed her clothes, putting on a red woollen dress, very plain and severely tailored, flattering her slim figure. So how could marriage ever be open? Commitment meant promising to be loyal and faithful to the person you liked living with, liked being with; the person you loved. It meant putting that other person before yourself. Well, she had tried to do that, hadn't she? But had Alun?

Wearing a straight black woollen coat over her dress, a silk scarf tucked into its neckline, and high-heeled shiny black boots, she was waiting for Chris when he entered. He looked really pleased to see her again, his broad face smiling.

'You look different somehow,' he said. 'More sure of yourself. Is it permitted to kiss you in greeting?'

'I think so,' she laughed, offering him a cheek. The brief embrace over, she tucked a hand through the crook of his arm and they walked to the door. 'You know, I have a feeling I'm going to enjoy myself this evening. I haven't been invited out to dinner for ages.'

Soon they were driving along wet lanes into the countryside. Winkleford was a tiny village situated at a crossroads; a cluster of old cottages around a tall-towered Norman church. Opposite to the church on the other side of the village green was the inn, its stone walls glowing warmly in the lamplight, rose-coloured light slanting out from its mullioned windows.

Inside the same rose-coloured light shone on dark wooden panelling, on small round tables and old Windsor chairs. A fire flickered in a huge stone fireplace.

'This is nice,' said Jessica appreciatively as after taking off her coat she sat down at the table to which they had been led by the hostess. 'How long have they been serving meals here?'

'They opened the dining room at the beginning of July,' replied Chris. 'They had a good summer. Of course the weather helped. It was a real scorcher, wasn't it?'

'I don't know. . . .' she whispered. 'I . . . I wasn't here.'

'God, I'm sorry,' he said sincerely. 'I'd forgotten how badly injured you were. The accident happened when you were coming back from Wales, didn't it? What were you doing there?'

'I . . . I went to see Alun. Don't you remember? You suggested I contacted him, so I went to see him.'

He didn't say anything immediately because a waitress, dressed in country clothes of a past era, long cotton gingham gown in blue and white check, with a mob cap on her head, brought them the menus and offered to bring them cocktails. When she had gone Chris said,

'I remember suggesting that you got in touch with him about a divorce, but I don't remember suggesting that you should go and see him.' He paused, frowning at the menu. 'Did you ask him . . . about a divorce?'

'Yes, and . . . and he said I could go ahead and divorce him if I wanted to. I . . . I was late leaving his place and had to drive all night to get back because I knew that the bank would foreclose if Mother and I didn't come up with some plan. I phoned you from Dolgellau to tell you I'd decided to agree to your conditions if you would save Martin and Son Ltd. But you weren't there. You didn't answer.'

'When did you phone?' he asked.

'Soon after six. It was a Thursday evening. You said you'd be back then.'

'I didn't get back until the Saturday. There was a strike of air-line traffic controllers. They were working to rule and flights were delayed,' he explained easily. 'By the time I did get back your mother had sold out to Lithgow.' His mouth twisted. 'Just as well she did. I couldn't have helped you out of the mess you were in, as it turned out.'

'Oh, why is that?'

'My own company ran into a spot of bother, financially speaking, and we had to cut back, sack a lot of people and re-plan our whole operation, so there was no way I could have arranged to amalgamate with Martins. But I'm glad to say we're coming out of that recession now.'

They ordered their choice of food and the waitress went away again. Chris poured wine into their glasses.

'So what are you doing now?' he asked. 'Working for Lithgow?'

'Yes. At the Martin offices.'

'How's it going?'

'Not very well.'

'Oh. Why not?'

'Arthur won't let me have any freedom to do my own thing in design,' explained Jessica. 'I have to follow the Lithgow line all the time and sometimes I feel that he's only kept me on as a sort of sop, if you know what I mean?'

'I can guess,' replied Chris with a slight but

knowing grin. 'He doesn't want you going to work for another company because you just might be good at what you do. How about coming to work for Pollet's?'

She studied him across the table, wondering what lay behind his offer.

'Can you afford me?' she parried.

'I'll offer you more than Lithgow is paying you,' he retorted. 'Not much more but definitely more. Pollet's needs a new design right now to put the company at the top.'

'To beat Lithgows, you mean?'

'Exactly.' He leaned across the table. His grey eyes bored into hers. 'Come to Pollet's, Jess, and you can have all the freedom you want to design.'

She was tempted, but wary of him.

'Can I think about it?'

'Sure. Take your time. You came out to enjoy yourself, remember, so we won't talk shop any more.'

'But before we stop talking shop could I just ask you one question?' queried Jessica.

'Go ahead.'

'Would there be any conditions attached to your offer?'

'Conditions?' he scowled.

'Yes. Last time you offered something, when you offered to amalgamate with Martins and make me your partner, you said you would only do it if . . . if I divorced Alun. You said you didn't want him turning up and making claims on me. Remember?'

'Of course I remember,' he said rather irritably.

'But surely that doesn't apply now.' His glance sharpened. 'You're not telling me he's still around, are you?' He looked down at her left hand that was holding her glass. Light winked on the thick gold band on her third finger. 'Dammit, I didn't notice it before,' he muttered, then flicked her an underbrowed glance. 'You're still married to him?'

'Yes, I'm still married to him.'

'But you said you're living alone at the flat.'

'I am. He ... Alun is away, on assignment for the magazine.'

'But you're divorcing him, aren't you? You've filed for a divorce?' Chris demanded sharply.

'No.'

'Why not?'

'I ... well, we still have to discuss it,' she faltered.

'But I thought you went to Wales to do that?'

'I did ... but since then ... since I got better from the accident he and I ... we've lived together for a short while.'

'I see.' He spoke through tight lips, his eyes wintry and leaned back, away from her.

'You haven't answered my question, Chris. Would you insist on my divorcing Alun if I take the job you're offering?'

He gave her a narrowed assessing stare across the table before answering slowly and thoughtfully.

'No, I wouldn't insist,' he said. 'Not this time. That make it easier for you to decide?'

'Yes,' she said, showing her relief by smiling at

him. 'Much easier. Now let's stop talking shop and enjoy ourselves.'

It was just after ten o'clock when the car drew up outside the block of flats. They had been talking furniture design on the way back from the inn and before she opened the car door Jessica turned to Chris and said,

'Would you like to come up to the flat and see the drawings I've been talking about? The designs I've made for the chairs I'd like to have in the flat if only I could get them made?'

'Yes, I would,' he agreed with alacrity.

He parked the car and they went up to the sixth floor in the lift together. In the kitchenette of the flat Jessica put the coffee-maker on while he sat in the small dining area and studied the drawings she had made for chairs.

'Well? What do you think?' she asked when the coffee was made and she had carried a tray bearing two mugs, cream and sugar and the pot into the living part of the big room and had set it down on the coffee table. She sat down on the couch and began to pour coffee.

'I think you're a very clever designer,' said Chris, coming to sit down beside her. 'And that given the freedom to create in your own way you could become a name in furniture design.' He took the coffee mug she offered him from her and set it down on the table, then turned to her, and she became aware how close he was sitting. 'I also think you're beautiful, Jess,' he whispered. 'And I can't promise that if you come to work for me I'll be able to keep my hands off you. What are your feelings about sexual harassment on the job?'

He leaned closer to her, his eyes hooded, their glance directed deliberately and suggestively to her lips. He wanted to kiss her, make love to her. *Why not? Why not?* a voice taunted within her. *Let him. You're an adult, and what two consenting adults do in private is their business.* Her lips parted in invitation.

As soon as his lips touched hers she closed her eyes and imagined she was being kissed by Alun, that they were Alun's arms that were around her, Alun's fingers easing undone the zip at the back of her dress.

A bell rang imperatively, and Chris lifted his lips from hers and frowned down at her.

'Are you expecting someone?' he asked.

'No.' She moved away from him, pushing back her hair. 'Perhaps it was next door's.'

The bell rang again, several times, as if someone was jabbing at it with an impatient finger.

'It is yours,' said Chris, standing up. 'Shall I go?'

'No ... no, it's all right. Might be one of the neighbours. Stay here, I'll answer the door.'

Jessica stepped out into the small hallway. The bell rang again. She opened the door, aware that Chris had followed her, wishing he hadn't. She didn't want whoever was at the door to see him. The door swung back.

'I was just beginning to think you weren't in or that I'd come to the wrong door,' said Alun, and walked right past her into the hallway as if he owned the place.

'Oh!' Pure delight that he had come to her, that he was there, actually there in the hallway, danced through her like a shower of golden sparks, lighting up her mind, her body. 'I wasn't expecting you,' she added hastily, noticing him staring at Chris.

'No?' He looked back at her, frowning. Deeply tanned, his hair a wild tangle, a growth of black beard on his cheeks and chin, he looked as if he had come straight from the rain forest to London, for he was wearing tough greenish bush clothes. 'But I sent you a card to say I'd be here today,' he said.

'When? When did you send it, and from where?'

'Last week from New Guinea.'

'It hasn't arrived yet. But how did you know my address?'

'I didn't. I sent it to Wordsworth Close—I've just come from there. Your mother told me about this place.' He glanced again at Chris.

'This ... this is Chris Pollet, a friend of mine,' said Jessica hastily. 'Chris, this is Alun Gower.'

'Hi, Chris,' said Alun casually, humping his travelling bag before him as he edged past Chris and into the living room. 'Excuse me, I'd like to dump my things somewhere, and grab a shave and a shower.'

He went through the living room, finding his way unerringly to the passage that led to the bathroom and the bedroom, as if he had lived there before. Chris and Jessica stood and looked at each other.

'I'll get out of your way,' murmured Chris, picking up his thick woollen car-coat and slipping it on over his suit. 'You'll let me know if you want to come and work for me?'

'Yes ... yes, I'll let you know,' she muttered, following him to the flat entrance. 'Thank you for dinner. I enjoyed it very much. Goodnight, Chris.'

'Goodnight, Jess.'

The door closed behind him. Jessica stood for a moment listening to the wild beating of her heart, feeling flames burning in her cheeks. Alun had come back and had found her with another man. Now what?

She went into the living room and, picking up the mug Chris had taken, put it on the tray. Then she carried the tray into the kitchenette. She emptied both mugs of the coffee they contained and rinsed them out. Then she went along to the bedroom. The bathroom door was closed when she passed it and she assumed Alun was in there.

The clothes he had been wearing were lying on the pale thick carpet of the bedroom where he had dropped them. She picked them up, wrinkling her nose distastefully at the smell of them, and dropped them into the wicker clothes basket. Then she undressed, putting her dress away on a hanger in the closet. Her slip and other underwear went into the clothes basket. Taking a housecoat made from dark blue silk, she slipped it on and zipped it up, then pushed her feet into mules made from soft blue velveteen. And all the time her heart was

singing because Alun had come back. He had
come to her first. He hadn't gone to Wales.

'Jessica?' The bathroom door had opened and
he was shouting, 'Is this towel the best you can
provide? Don't you have anything bigger? It
wouldn't dry a pygmy!'

Suddenly she was scurrying about, out into the
passage to the linen closet. She had forgotten she
had put the bath-towel she had used earlier in the
dirty clothes basket and hadn't replaced it. She
went to the bathroom door. It was partly open,
steam floating through the opening and out into
the passage. She stepped into the room, thinking
that Alun was still in the bath, behind the shower
curtain.

'I've hung it on the rail,' she said.

'Thanks,' he said from behind her, and before
she could whirl to face him he put his arms around
her and dragged her back against him, holding her
captive.

'Oh, what do you think you're doing!' she gasped,
her hands on his brawny bare arms. 'Let me go!'

'Not until you tell me what you and Pollet were
doing,' he growled, putting his head down beside
hers, his curls tickling her temple, his breath hot
against her ear and then his teeth nibbling the
lobe, biting it sharply so that she squeaked.

'We . . . we weren't doing anything,' she gasped.
'I . . . he's in furniture too and he was looking at
some designs of mine.'

'Oh, sure,' he jeered. 'Then why did you and he
both have a guilty look on your faces as if you'd
been caught in the act?'

'What act?' she asked in all innocence.

'Oh, come on, Jess,' Alun drawled with a touch of weariness. 'You know what I mean. *I* haven't *lost* my memory. I know damned well he's the guy who wanted to marry you. He's your lover, isn't he.'

'No, he isn't!' Jessica spat the words out as she tried to struggle free of his hold. 'Alun, let go of me—please! Oh, what are you doing now?'

'Undressing you. I have the right to, you know,' he asserted arrogantly. Even while she had struggled he had managed to unzip the housecoat. 'We'll finish this in the shower,' he added, lifting her, his hands at her waist.

'No!' she shrieked, feeling completely helpless, lifted that way in front of him, her mules falling off as she kicked her feet frantically. 'Put me down—put me down at once!'

'Certainly,' Alun said scoffingly, putting her down in the bath and stepping in too, still behind her, holding her against him with one arm while he pulled the shower curtain across and then turned on the shower.

'Oh, no!' she yelled. 'My housecoat will be ruined! You devil—you mischievous fiend! What do you think you're doing?'

'Trying to find out the truth about you and Pollet,' he retorted, and as her housecoat slid down to lie in a wet pool at her feet he spun her round to face him while warm water sluiced over them. His fingers bit bruisingly into the soft flesh of her upper arms as he glared down at her. 'Was he making love to you when I rang the door-bell?' he demanded.

'He . . . he was kissing me, yes. Alun, this is silly, standing like this, getting wet.'

'Is it? I'm finding it rather stimulating.' Pulling her close to him, he rubbed himself against her intimately and she felt desire spring up in her. 'And if I hadn't come when I did would it have gone further than just kissing?' he demanded, his voice hoarse as he continued to hold her closely, his fingertips walking lightly over her warm skin that had been sensitised by the tingling spray of water so that every delicate nerve ending was alive and aching for his touch. Delicious sensations shot through her. Her head reeling, she groaned in pleasurable agony, wanting to feel more, and she had to lean against his hard wet body for support.

'You're jealous,' she accused gaspingly, delighted that he could be.

'I'll admit to jealousy when I know if I have any reason to be jealous,' Alun whispered menacingly. 'Now answer my question.' His hands slid along her shoulders threateningly to curve about her throat. His thumbs tantalised the pulse in the vulnerable hollow at the base. 'Would it have gone any further if I hadn't arrived when I did?'

'I don't know,' she moaned. 'I was feeling so lonely and I was longing for you. But he didn't kiss me like you do. No one has ever kissed me the way you do, or done the things you do to me.' His hands were sliding down from her throat to cup her taut breasts and his lips followed them, his wet curls tickling her already titillated skin. 'Oh, please do that again,' she whispered when his hard tongue licked one vulnerable pink point. 'Please kiss me there again. It makes me feel so. . . .' She groaned in ecstasy.

'So what?' he asked.

'So happy to be with you again.' Jessica rubbed herself against him until he was groaning too. 'Are we going to do it here?'

'If you want to do it.' Alun's voice was thick with passion.

'I want to do it . . . now,' she sighed, arching her body like a bow ready for an arrow to the thrust of his desire.

A long time later, when they had dried each other with thick soft towels, and were curled up in bed together, they talked sleepily in the darkness.

'I was so worried in case you went to Wales first, in case you didn't come back to me,' Jessica admitted.

'Why would I go to Wales first?' he asked.

'To . . . to see Mavis Owen.'

'Now why the hell would I want to go and see her?' he spoke more sharply, no longer sleepy.

'You used to be in love with her, before she married Gareth. She told me you and she had fallen in love again and wanted to start an adventure school together.'

'Poppycock,' he said abruptly.

'What did you say?'

'I said poppycock—a good English slang word for nonsense. I was never in love with Mavis Owen and she never attracted me. And I never want to start an adventure school with her as my partner.'

'But she said you'd told her that you could only

go into partnership with her if you weren't married to me,' she argued. 'And when I asked you if you'd said that to her you admitted that you had.'

'I told her I couldn't be her partner while I was married to you to stop her from pestering me,' he growled. 'I was sick and tired of her going on about the bloody adventure school and how great it would be if she and I were partners. That didn't mean I didn't want to be married to you. I was using my marriage to you as a protection against her.'

'Oh. I . . . I thought you wanted a divorce,' said Jessica weakly.

'It was you who came asking for a divorce,' he retorted.

'And you said I could have one if it was what I wanted,' she retaliated, 'so when Mavis told me what you'd said to her I thought being married to me was getting in your way, preventing you from doing something that she said had been your dream; a dream you'd shared with her and Gareth, to start an adventure school.'

'That was their dream, but never mine,' said Alun. 'I'd never have gone into a business partnership with either of them. Both of them were unreliable.'

'Aren't you going to start an adventure school, then?'

'No, I'm not.'

'Then what are you going to do with the farm?'

'I've already done it. While you were lying in a coma in hospital I arranged for the farm to be amalgamated with Dai Jones's farm, with him in charge.' He paused, then asked slowly, 'Did you really believe what Mavis said, that our marriage was getting in my way?'

'It wasn't hard to believe. I knew, you see, that you'd never really wanted to be married and that you'd only married me to help me to convince my father I didn't want to and wouldn't marry Arthur Lithgow. *Ouch!* Alun, stop pulling my hair—it hurts!'

'I'm trying to stop you from talking poppycock,' he muttered, leaning over her. 'Now listen to me, really listen, I mean, and take in what I'm going to say to you, because I might never feel like saying it again. I married you because I wanted to marry you. I wanted you to be mine and only mine. I admit I had a few qualms about giving up my freedom, but you seemed to be willing to go along with the idea of me going away often, and we were doing pretty well until you started listening to Sally.'

'Well, how was I supposed to know Ashley King was your mother and not your lover?' she retorted. 'You never told me anything about your family.'

'My mistake.' The bitterness in his voice was directed at himself. 'I know that now. I should have explained to you, but instead I lost my temper. I was hurt, see? I was hurt because you didn't trust me the way I trusted you; because you were willing to listen to Sally's jealous tales about me and believe them. And she was jealous of you, you know. She was jealous because I preferred you to her.'

He flung himself back on his pillow. There was a long silence. The only sounds were the quickened throbs of both their hearts. After a while Jessica said forlornly,

'If only you'd come back to me when you returned from that expedition to the Canadian Arctic! If only you'd written, or phoned, or done something to communicate with me.'

'If only you'd been living at our flat when I did return,' he replied gruffly. 'But you weren't and I was hurt again believing that you'd had enough of our rather fragile marriage.'

'I missed you so much during those two years,' she whispered, snuggling closer to him. Alun raised an arm and put it around her shoulders and gathered her against him. She rested her head on his shoulder.

'I missed you too,' he replied. 'And when you did turn up at Whitewalls I was so excited that I did and said all the wrong things, frightened you away.'

'It wasn't you who frightened me away, it was Mavis. But I had to leave—I couldn't stay. I had to go back to help Mother.'

'I know you did. I understood that, but now, looking back, I realise I should have gone with you and then maybe you wouldn't have been in that accident....' Alun broke off and his arm tightened about her. 'If you knew how I felt when I got your mother's letter telling me you'd been badly hurt, that you couldn't walk and had lost your memory, you'd have no doubts about my feelings for you,' he said in a low shaken voice. 'It's a good thing your mother wasn't there in person. I'd have hit her, I think for not letting me know sooner. All that time I'd been waiting to hear that you'd filed for a divorce you'd been lying in a coma, and I hadn't known.' He drew in a long breath. 'If you'd changed your name when we got married; if you'd had something on you that had shown the police that as your husband I was your next of kin and should have been informed of any accident, I'd have known before your mother.'

'Did she ever tell you why she hadn't let you know sooner?' asked Jessica.

'She said she'd hesitated because she didn't know how things were between you and me, and also that she wasn't at all sure where I lived in Wales. She apologised for not being in touch sooner and then went on to lecture me about my responsibilities as a husband, how I should take care of you, stay with you while you were learning to walk again, help you to regain your memory.' He laughed. 'She's a very sweet lady, so I followed her advice and took you away to King's Fancy, where you pretended your memory hadn't returned, God knows why.'

'I was afraid,' she whispered. 'I was afraid you were only staying with me because it's what a husband is expected to do and not what you wanted to do.'

'Little cheat,' Alun taunted softly, hugging her again.

'Well, you didn't seem to want me any more. You slept in another room and you didn't make love to me.'

'Because I thought you wouldn't want me to,' he replied and again bitterness edged his voice. 'The last time I'd tried you'd pushed me away and had asked me not to touch you, giving me the impression that being made love to by me was the last thing you wanted. Lust, you called it, and said it didn't mean anything.'

'I said that because I was never sure, you see, that you wanted me because you loved me,' she confessed.

'I loved you and I still love you. I've loved you ever since I met you in the Fairbourne's House and you stood there in your riding clothes, with your hair about your shoulders, and looked down your nose at me.'

'I didn't look down my nose at you,' she gasped, amazed at this view he had had of her.

'Oh yes, you did. You're always looking down your nose at me as if you're the superior princess in a fairy tale and I'm the beggar in the gutter. That's been your challenge to me always.'

'I didn't know,' Jessica said weakly.

'I had to wait a few years for you to grow up and then you played right into my hands,' he said with a note of triumph. 'Why do you think I took you in, gave you shelter and found you a job? Because I loved you and wanted you. If I hadn't I wouldn't have done a damn thing for you. I'm not the stuff of which knight errants are made, you know. I don't give help to every damsel in distress who comes my way. Only to you.'

'Oh, I wish I'd known. I wish you'd told me,' she groaned. 'I suppose you think now that I've behaved in a very silly way.'

'There have been moments when I've wondered

about you,' Alun admitted dryly, 'wondered whether you would ever come to terms with yourself.'

'Would you like to know why?' she asked, raising a hand to touch his face, tracing the line of his lips until he opened them and snapped his teeth at her finger so that she snatched it away.

'As long as it doesn't take too long,' he drawled. 'I'm beginning to feel lustful again.'

'I . . . I've never been sure that you loved me,' she murmured. 'I could never see what it was that you . . . or someone like you, so strong and clever and adventurous, and free-spirited—could see in me, an ordinary conventional woman who likes houses and furniture and flowers and who would like so much to have babies, at least two, and would stay at home to look after them.'

'Didn't it ever occur to you that I love you because you are like that? Because you're so very different from any other woman I've known well? Because you're generous and kind and fairly good-humoured?' Turning on to his side, he held her closely to him. 'I love you, I want you,' he whispered thickly. 'For me the two go together. I can't separate them. I can only make love to you because I love only you. Do you get the message?'

'I think so. Oh, Alun, what a good thing you came back today! I might have done something else very silly if you hadn't.'

'Such as?' he demanded, his voice soft and sibilant with menace.

'I . . . I'll tell you another time,' stammered Jessica, hastily backing away from telling him she had been close to submitting to Chris Pollet's lovemaking. 'It wasn't very important,' she added, sensing that he wasn't satisfied with her answer. 'Not as important as the way I feel about you.' She arched her body to the touch of his hands. 'Alun, please say you'll always come back to me, when you've been away?'

'I'll always come back to you, that is if you'll have me,' he vowed, sounding rather humble for him.

'I'll have you. I'll always have you. I want you to be a part of my life always,' she vowed in her turn. 'I want to have your children and no one else's. I want to create a home for us and them, for you to come back to.'

'And that's what I want too, my golden girl, my shining gift,' he whispered. 'Always have wanted and always will.'

And as the last mists that had shrouded their love for each other, hiding their real feelings from each other, lifted and floated away, their love blazed up, a pure white flame consuming all doubts and inhibitions and lighting the way to the complete fulfilment of all their desires.

Take these
4 best-selling novels
FREE

Yes! Four sophisticated, contemporary love stories by four world-famous authors of romance FREE, as your introduction to the Harlequin Presents subscription plan. Thrill to **Anne Mather**'s passionate story BORN OUT OF LOVE, set in the Caribbean.... Travel to darkest Africa in **Violet Winspear**'s TIME OF THE TEMPTRESS.... Let **Charlotte Lamb** take you to the fascinating world of London's Fleet Street in MAN'S WORLD.... Discover beautiful Greece in **Sally Wentworth**'s moving romance SAY HELLO TO YESTERDAY.

Harlequin Presents...

The very finest in romance fiction

Join the millions of avid Harlequin readers all over the world who delight in the magic of a really exciting novel. EIGHT great NEW titles published EACH MONTH! Each month you will get to know exciting, interesting, true-to-life people .... You'll be swept to distant lands you've dreamed of visiting .... Intrigue, adventure, romance, and the destiny of many lives will thrill you through each Harlequin Presents novel.

Get all the latest books before they're sold out!
As a Harlequin subscriber you actually receive your personal copies of the latest Presents novels immediately after they come off the press, so you're sure of getting all 8 each month.

Cancel your subscription whenever you wish!
You don't have to buy any minimum number of books. Whenever you decide to stop your subscription just let us know and we'll cancel all further shipments.

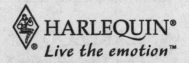

HARLEQUIN® *Temptation.*

AMERICAN HEROES

These men are heroes—
strong, fearless...
And impossible to resist!

Join bestselling authors Lori Foster, Donna Kauffman
and Jill Shalvis as they deliver up

MEN OF COURAGE

**Harlequin anthology
May 2003**

Followed by *American Heroes* miniseries
in Harlequin Temptation

**RILEY by Lori Foster
June 2003**

**SEAN by Donna Kauffman
July 2003**

**LUKE by Jill Shalvis
August 2003**

Don't miss this sexy new miniseries by some of
Temptation's hottest authors!

Available at your favorite retail outlet.

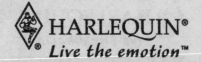

HARLEQUIN®
Live the emotion™

Visit us at www.eHarlequin.com

HTAH

eHARLEQUIN.com

For great romance books at great prices,
shop www.eHarlequin.com today!

GREAT BOOKS:
- **Extensive selection** of today's hottest
  books, including **current** releases,
  backlist titles and new **upcoming** books.
- **Favorite authors:** Nora Roberts,
  Debbie Macomber and more!

GREAT DEALS:
- **Save every day:** enjoy great savings
  and special online promotions.
- *Exclusive* **online offers:** FREE books,
  bargain outlet savings, special deals.

EASY SHOPPING:
- Easy, secure, **24-hour shopping** from the
  comfort of your own home.
- **Excerpts, reader recommendations**
  and our **Romance Legend** will help
  you choose!
- **Convenient shipping and
  payment methods.**

Shop online
at www.eHarlequin.com today!

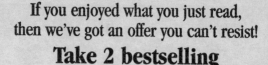

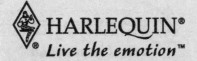

Blaze

HARLEQUIN® *Blaze*™

Rory Carmichael is a good girl, trying to survive the suburbs.
Micki Carmichael is a bad girl, trying to survive the streets.
Both are about to receive an invitation
they won't be able to refuse....

INVITATIONS TO SEDUCTION

Enjoy this Blazing duo by fan favorite
Julie Elizabeth Leto:

#92—LOOKING FOR TROUBLE
June 2003

#100—UP TO NO GOOD
August 2003

And don't forget to pick up

INVITATIONS TO SEDUCTION

the 2003 Blaze collection
by Vicki Lewis Thompson,
Carly Phillips and Janelle Denison
Available July 2003

Summers can't get any hotter than this!

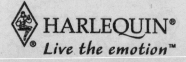

HARLEQUIN®
Live the emotion™